ONE HUNDRED EXCUSES

AN ASPEN COVE SMALL TOWN ROMANCE

KELLY COLLINS

BOOK NOOK PRESS

CHAPTER ONE

Blackmail is a dirty word...a crime, really, unless you're doing it to stop something much worse.

Marina Caswell was certain of three things in life. The first was Lord Acton had it right when he said, "Absolute power corrupts absolutely." The second was, all the good men were married or dead. Lastly, she'd do anything to protect her daughter —anything.

Marina sat on the worn plaid couch in the middle of the living room. It wasn't much, but it was free, and free was what she could afford.

The tiny bungalow was small and filled with a wall of boxes—boxes that should contain the memories of a beautiful life and not the remnants of a painful past. It was a new beginning, and from nothing, she'd make something. She had to for Kellyn.

"Hey, Ladybug, are you hungry?" She looked at her daughter's sweet little face and thanked her lucky stars they'd escaped.

Big brown eyes looked up at her through a fringe of dark chocolate hair, and Marina saw gratefulness in the four-year-old's expression. Little Kellyn Caswell had walked through hell and come out on the other side.

"Let's get a muffin. I know a lady in town that makes the best baked goods within a hundred miles." Marina rolled from the couch to her feet and offered Kellyn her hand. They made it to the door when Kellyn ran back to get her Mrs. Beasley doll.

It warmed Marina's heart that the old doll had become her daughter's favorite. It had been Marina's mom's doll, and then hers, and now Kellyn's. The blue and white polka-dotted dress had dried lots of tears and given lots of hugs. Gone were the black-rimmed spectacles. The blonde hair had thinned to bald in a few places, but she was a beloved friend to three generations—a grandma doll loved by all.

"That's right, you can't leave Mrs. Beasley behind. She'll want her tea."

Marina pulled the string, and the doll spoke. "Long ago, I was a little girl just like you," it said.

Kellyn hugged Mrs. Beasley tightly to her chest and followed Marina outside.

They walked into the sun, and the heat of the rays was like a kiss from the universe. The first day of their new life lay before them.

Aspen Cove was tucked between Long's Peak and Mount Meeker. The surrounding landscape hugged the tiny mountain town.

On Jasmine Lane sat their little house. It wasn't much, but it was affordable. It would only take a few haircuts a month and a coloring or two to keep a roof over their heads and food in their bellies. It wasn't the life she dreamed of for her and her daughter, but it was the life they had, and Marina would make sure it was a life worth living. She refused to be a victim and chose the path that made her a victor.

She wanted nothing from the man she'd believed was her white knight. Turned out Craig didn't ride a horse and wield a sword. He drove a Mercedes and swung his fist. The money he would reluctantly pay in child support was needed for Kellyn. He owed that much if not more to his daughter. Something told Marina it was more—way more.

She lifted Kellyn into her booster seat and buckled her in. Thank God she'd been able to talk Craig's parents into giving her their old car. It was funny how a two-year-old SUV was old to them but new to her. The Caswells' loss was her gain. They liked perfection, and the minute the housekeeper backed into it, no one drove it again. In their minds, anything needing fixing wasn't worth their time. It was probably why they didn't argue when she demanded full custody of Kellyn, a little girl who held none of her DNA but all of her heart. It also didn't hurt that she had a video of Craig at his worst. Mayor Caswell's run for reelection couldn't have come at a better time.

Marina was about to hop into the driver's seat when a police car pulled into the driveway next door. A dark-haired man stepped out and walked toward her. His shadow ate up the sun that had once provided welcome warmth. Surely their freedom hadn't come to an end already?

"Stay here, sweetie. I'll be right back." Marina closed her door and met the uniformed man halfway. "Can I help you?" Her spine was steel straight. Her heart beat like the wings of a hummingbird inside the hollow cage of her chest.

"Welcome to the neighborhood," the man said. When he smiled, the hard edges of his face softened. It would be so easy to get pulled in by a smiling face. That's what had happened two years ago when she met Craig. He'd come in for a haircut and left with her number. After she met his daughter, the rest was history.

"Thank you—" she looked down at his name tag "—Sheriff Cooper." She wondered if this was simply a friendly hello or her ex-brother-in-law flexing his muscles through his connections.

"I'm your neighbor." He pointed to the cute white bungalow next door. Where hers had peeling paint and a yard that hadn't seen a mower in years, his was picture-perfect, down to the flower boxes under the windows and the rocker on the front porch.

"Oh, okay. I'm Marina." She figured he'd already know that piece of information.

"Nice to meet you, Marina. If you need anything, don't be afraid to ask. I'm happy to help in any way I can." He held out his hand, and she stared at it for a slow second. How long had it been since a man's hand offered something other than agony?

She gave him a solid shake and smiled. "Thanks, Sheriff." She glanced over her shoulder to where Kellyn had her face pressed against the glass. Terror danced in her baby's eyes. "We're good, but I'll let you know if I need something."

She turned around and walked back to the SUV. She could feel him looking at her—the heat of his stare at her back. She hated that she had to question the intentions of all men, but that's what being married to the devil had caused.

She opened her daughter's door and squatted in front of the frightened child. "It's okay, honey." She brushed away the tears that ran down Kellyn's cheeks. "He's a good guy." Lord, she hoped she was right. He seemed like one of the good ones. She never wanted to lie to her baby. "Not all men are bad or mean or hurt people." Maybe she should listen to her own advice. Her ability to trust was at an all-time low, and she didn't know if she would be about to trust again. "Let's get that muffin, okay?"

Five minutes later, they were parked on Main Street in front of B's Bakery. Had it really been months since she'd been here?

There was a line inside three-deep, so hand in hand, Marina and Kellyn waited their turn. When they got to the front, the little blonde standing behind the glass display case squealed with delight.

"Oh my God, you're back." She raced around the counter and pulled Marina in for a big hug, then pulled back to look at her. No doubt she was searching for cuts and bruises—a staple in Marina's old wardrobe. "I wondered what happened to you." She looked down at Kellyn. "Who's this?"

"My daughter," Marina said with pride.

"You have a daughter?"

Marina moved Kellyn, who had hid behind her legs, to the front. "This is Kellyn. She's four." She pointed to the doll. "This is Mrs. Beasley, and she's about forty or so. We came for tea and muffins."

"Hi, Kellyn, I'm Katie Bishop. Let's have a tea party, okay?" She looked at Kellyn and waited for an answer.

Marina smiled. "Kellyn doesn't talk."

"Oh. Can she—" Katie pointed to her ear.

"She can hear you. She's a great listener, and it's not that she can't talk. There's nothing physically wrong with her. She chooses not to talk."

Katie smiled. "Conversation is overrated. Why talk when we can have tea and eat carrot cake muffins?" She turned to leave but stopped and kneeled in front of Kellyn. "Do you really want tea, or would you rather have chocolate milk?"

Kellyn's eyes opened wide, and her rosy lips lifted into a smile.

"Chocolate milk it is." Katie disappeared behind the counter while Marina pulled colored wood cylinders from her bag. One green. One yellow. One red. She sat them in front of Kellyn. "You doing all right, Ladybug?"

Kellyn grabbed the green and stood it up while the others lay on their sides.

"Good, I'm so happy. You're going to like it here, and someday, you'll feel safe enough to tell me everything." She pressed her lips to her daughter's forehead. "I love you so much."

Katie rounded the counter with a tray full of goodies. She set it down and went to the corner to get two booster seats, one for Kellyn and one for her doll.

The four of them sat around a small metal bistro table and chatted. Though Mrs. Beasley and Kellyn said nothing, Marina knew that one of them was paying close attention. Kellyn might be silent, but she was far from unobservant. She often wondered if somehow she stayed mute to enhance her other skills. Was it a survival mechanism?

"I had no idea you were a mother."

Marina pulled a coloring book and crayons from her bag and set them in front of Kellyn. It was funny how her purse became a clown car once she became a parent. She could reach inside a dozen times and pull something out to entertain her child.

"Yes, Kellyn is my ex's daughter, but I have full custody of her since last week."

Katie's look of surprise told Marina she recognized how unusual their situation was. "He's…" There were so many questions in her big blue eyes.

"Still in Copper Creek." She looked at Kellyn, who was busy coloring, and lowered her voice to a whisper. "He's still running the permits department. His father is still the mayor. His older brother is the chief of police. His younger brother is the district attorney. It's been a challenge."

Marina looked at the wall beyond them. Hanging in the center was a corkboard called The Wishing Wall. It was where she'd put her wish for a plan B the last time she sat in the bakery feeling beaten, not by Craig's fists, but by the power of his family. That wish was granted when local multimillionaire musician Samantha White, also known as Indigo, hired her to color her hair and insisted on overpaying her. It was the turning point in Marina's and Kellyn's lives. The money allowed her to buy the nanny cam that caught Craig in action.

She shuddered to think about that day. The day she didn't fight back. She stood and took every hit, knowing they would be his last.

"I can't imagine." Katie looked at Kellyn. It was obvious how sweet and caring a woman she was. Anyone with a wishing wall couldn't be half bad.

"You have to live it to believe it."

Katie pointed to the Lego table in the corner. "She's welcome to play."

Kellyn's eyes lit up.

"Go ahead, sweetie. I'll be right here."

Kellyn grabbed her green cylinder from the table and went to play.

"She's feeling safe."

Marina knew there would be questions. Everyone had questions, but few people had answers.

"She's safe here. You're safe here. We take care of our own. You must be the single mom Lydia mentioned at her wedding."

"Dr. Nichols is wonderful."

"It's Dr. Covington now. She married Wes."

Marina's brow lifted. "I think I met her husband not too long ago in my husb…" She moved close to Katie and whispered. "Craig's office. He seemed nice."

"He's great. That means you're the single mom living next to Aiden."

Marina sipped her tea. "Is that Sheriff Cooper?"

"Yes. He's a great guy too."

"If you say so." She wasn't convinced there were any great guys left. Her experience was once men reached thirty, the only ones left were damaged or deadly.

Katie laid her hand on top of Marina's. "A girl could do a lot worse than Aiden. He's a solid guy."

Marina laughed. "Solid isn't a prerequisite. In fact, it's not even an attribute I'd find attractive. While I used to love men, I'm not sure having one in our lives is important at this point."

"You never know until the right one comes along." Katie's whole demeanor turned high-school-girl giddy. It was obvious she'd found a keeper.

"How do you know they're the right one?"

"Your heart will tell you."

The problem was Marina's heart had hardened to stone. It would take one hell of a man to tear down the walls she'd thrown up. The only one to penetrate the fortress was a four-year-old girl who'd been abandoned by her biological mother, terrorized by her biological father, and set aside by her grandparents because they deemed her imperfect.

CHAPTER TWO

Aiden watched the petite woman climb into her SUV and drive away. He knew without a doubt that Marina must be the single mother Dr. Lydia had told him about the day she got married to his friend Wes Covington. Aspen Cove had seen more weddings in the last year or so than it had probably seen in the last decade. Love was like a virus, and Lydia, one of the town's doctors, was certain he would be next to catch the bug.

He knew it was only a matter of time before he got a neighbor, and he was damned pleased he'd gotten one as pretty as her.

Aspen Cove was growing, and with growth came people. He was happy to see that some of them came as the fairer sex. All he'd seen so far were big men with bigger attitudes. With only a handful of single women in town, there was a lot of dick-swinging going on. In his experience, too much testosterone was like a powder keg, and jealousy was the flame.

He plucked a few weeds growing between the cracks in his walkway and headed for the front door. He was pulling a double shift since his deputy Mark Bancroft was out sick. With the Guild Creative Center and the firehouse being built, it was only a matter of time before they'd need more deputies. Right now, he'd settle for any help he could get.

Most people weren't looking for small-town work. Aiden wasn't looking for big-town problems. It was why he'd ended up in Aspen Cove several years ago. He loved his small-town life, but was afraid of the changes he knew were coming their way.

He turned the knob of his front door just as his house phone rang.

"Hey, Mom," he said with a smile to his voice as he picked up the handset.

"How'd you know it was me?" Sara Cooper asked.

"You're the only one who calls on the landline. In fact, I'm sure you're the only one who has that number. Most people use a cell phone."

He put his keys on the hallway table, walked into his kitchen, and opened the refrigerator. He couldn't wait for the grand opening of the new culinary school Dalton was building and, with it, the take-and-bake shop. That would go a long way in making sure he didn't eat spaghetti every day of the week. He pulled out a tub of noodles and a container of red sauce and put them on the counter. After a quick lunch, he'd head back to the office.

"Why do I need a cell phone when I have a perfectly good phone hanging on the wall?"

Aiden laughed. She still had a rotary dial phone in the kitchen. He'd spend ten minutes each time he was home unraveling the cord. "I'm done arguing the point. I bought you a phone, and you should use it." He'd be surprised if last year's Christmas gift wasn't still in its box.

"I'm saving it for when I really need it."

"When you really need it, it will still be in the box."

"Fine, but I didn't call you to talk about phones. I called to see if you're coming down this weekend."

He got a plate of pasta ready, dumped an ample amount of Parmesan cheese on top, and put it in the microwave.

He tried to visit his mother at least once a month. "Can't come this weekend. Mark is sick, so I'm picking up the slack."

"But Victoria will be back in town, and Mimi and I thought it would be great to get you two back together. I mean—"

"Mom," he warned. "Victoria and I aren't ever getting back together." Victoria was the last person Aiden wanted to see. They'd been engaged when he was injured four years ago. It was supposed to be a simple speeding ticket but turned into a high-speed chase and an exchange of gunfire.

"Oh, honey, you can't blame her for panicking. It's scary being married to a cop." Mom would know since her husband had been one for thirty years before his death. Aiden's dad had made it all the way through to retirement only to be killed by a drunk driver a week after he left the force.

"Nope, you're right. I can't blame her for being scared when I got shot. Hell, I was scared, but I can blame her for sleeping with my partner. If she wanted comfort, she could have found it in our bed. You and her mother need to stop meddling."

He knew he'd won the fight when there was silence on the other end.

"Okay, I'll stop pressing, but I don't think it's healthy for you to be thirty-six and single."

"What about you? It's not like you're ancient. At fifty-eight, you've got some living to do as well."

"I'm trying," she said, but there wasn't a hint of conviction in her voice.

15

"Me too." He hadn't been interested in anyone since the Victoria debacle, but he thought about Marina and smiled. "I've got a new neighbor. She seems nice. She has a child."

"Oh really? You like her?"

He could hear hope bloom in those two words. "Don't go ordering the wedding invitations. I've only just met her, but she seems nice enough." She was cordial but not overly friendly, and if he was being honest with himself, she seemed cautious. He'd caught a glimpse of her daughter and noticed the sheer look of panic on the little girl's face as she pressed her nose to the glass.

The way Marina stood between him and her child was telling. He knew right away she was a lioness ready to pounce if she thought her daughter was in danger. He liked that quality in a woman. Liked it when the people who were supposed to love you fought for you. Too bad Victoria didn't have that inside her. If she'd had that protective mechanism, their lives would have been a lot different. He might not be living in the tiny town of Aspen Cove. He would be in Colorado Springs, married and with a child or two of his own.

"Invite her over for your famous spaghetti," Mom suggested. "Women like men who can cook. Your dad got me with his beef stew."

"I'll keep that in mind." He took the steaming

plate out of the microwave. It was hot and cheesy, just the way he liked it." His cell phone rang. "Got to go. That's work calling."

"Love you," she said before hanging up.

"Hey, Poppy, what's up?" Poppy Dawson was in the office filing and answering the phones today.

"Sheriff Cooper, there's a problem at the firehouse. Something about a fight."

He looked at his lunch and groaned. Food would have to wait. "I'm on my way." He covered his dish with foil and raced out to his cruiser. The nice thing about small towns was he was minutes away from everything. At the same time, the problem with small towns was he was minutes from everything, which meant he never got away.

Three minutes later, he drove up to the new fire station. It was a work in progress, but it was coming along fast. The construction company was from Denver, so the men were used to a little more life in town, and if they couldn't find it, they created it.

He got out of his SUV and started toward the area where a group of men stood in a circle. One guy said, "Cops are here," as if warning the others to scatter like dust in the wind.

He could always tell the troublemakers because they seemed to grow larger as he got nearer as if their brawn could outwit his brain.

When he got to the center of the group, two

17

men were going at it like pugilists. "Break it up," he called out. He didn't want to step into a fight and hated that he might have to cuff someone and put them in a cell. He always tried to settle things with logic first.

"He started it," the bald guy yelled as he swiped blood from his lip.

Aiden wanted to roll his eyes. He was way beyond playground antics.

"You—" he pointed at the other man, who was fisted up and ready to swing "—need to stand down." He pointed to the pine tree off to the side. "Take your corner."

The man seemed to debate within himself. It took a single glance at Aiden's hand on his holster to make his decision and move to the tree.

After twenty minutes of talking to both men and finding out the fight was over a "borrowed lunch," Aiden headed to the diner, thinking he'd have a better chance of getting his stomach fed if he ordered the blue-plate special. Always hot. Always ready.

As he pulled into a parking spot, Marina was leaving the nearby bakery. He lifted his hand to wave, but she either didn't see him or she ignored the gesture.

He stood on the sidewalk, looking at her. What was her story?

Katie ran out of the shop with a bag in her hand. She passed it to the little girl who stood next to Marina. She was a pretty little thing with brown hair and eyes to match. She moved a green wooden cylinder from her right hand to her left and took the bag.

Katie threw her arms around Marina and gave her a kiss on the cheek. That wasn't the behavior to lavish on a woman she'd just met, but then again, it was Katie Bishop, and she lavished her love on everyone.

Aiden looked toward Maisey's Diner and decided that maybe today he'd settle for a carrot cake muffin.

He waited for the white Jeep to drive away before he walked inside the bakery.

"Hey, Coop." Katie was behind the counter filling half-empty trays. He loved the woman she'd grown into since she moved to Aspen Cove. He could still remember the frightened girl she was the day she showed up and took over the bakery. A bakery she had no idea how to run or any idea why Bea Bennett, a stranger, would have left it to her. It was amazing how much a town could change a person and how much a person could change a town. He'd delivered her first batch of muffin ingredients and left them anonymously at her door. It was a dying woman's wish that he couldn't ignore.

"I'll take a muffin, a coffee, and any information you have on our newest resident." He put a five on the counter and moved to the table in front of the window. He had a habit of sitting where he had the best view.

"You mean Marina?"

"Yes, she's my neighbor."

"She said she met you, and she's renting Doc's bungalow."

It was funny to hear the house next door called Doc's bungalow. No one had lived there since Doc's wife had died and his daughter moved out of town. Hell, he wouldn't have known it was Doc's if people in town hadn't told him, but then again, towns like Aspen Cove were that way. If you wanted to visit the Covingtons, you didn't say you were going to 10 Rose Lane. You said you were going to the big Victorian. If you wanted to see Sage and Cannon, you were going to the B and B. Bowie and Katie were the house next to the B and B, and Dalton and Samantha were the house next to last year's fire. Aiden lived next to Doc Parker's house, and no doubt people would say Marina lived next to the sheriff's house.

"You hugged her like you know her. Do you?"

Katie brought over his muffin and coffee and took the seat across from him. "She's been in town a few times."

He paid attention to the way she avoided eye contact. "What aren't you telling me?"

Her eyes got saucer big. "Nothing. I don't know much about her. Heck, I didn't know she had a daughter."

Aiden took a bite of his muffin and considered Marina for a minute. "What's her last name?"

Katie shrugged, "All I know is she's had a rough life. Her ex..." She chewed her lower lip. "He's the worst kind of man."

"Got a name?"

"Marina. That's her name. Her daughter is Kellyn."

"I know her name's Marina. What's her last name?"

"Last time I checked, I wasn't your deputy." She smiled. "I'm sure she'd tell you if you asked."

He knew Katie had more to offer, but she wasn't telling. He also knew that all it would take was a license plate check to find out all he needed to know about the beautiful Marina. He supposed if he wanted to get to know her better, he should go about it the right way. Most people didn't take kindly to him doing a full background check after the first hello.

CHAPTER THREE

She'd dropped the last chocolate chip onto the pancake and smiled. Kellyn wouldn't care that one eye was lower than the other. All she cared about was that the pancake was smiling and it contained chocolate.

Marina had Dr. Lydia to blame for Kellyn's new smiley face obsession and only herself to blame for the chocolate chip pancakes.

She flipped the single plate-sized cake and looked out the back window. Movement to her right caught her eye. Her heart raced like it could escape her chest. She hated that reaction. Hated herself for fearing every shadow and sound.

"I am a victor," she said to herself. "I fear nothing and no one." She leaned forward to see what had moved and caught the spray of a hose on the beautiful flowers next door. Only a short chain-link fence separated the houses. Sheriff Cooper was watering his garden.

She hadn't really gotten a good look at the man. He was a puzzle to her. Here was a man who carried a gun, wore a uniform, no doubt could throw a brutal punch, and yet he grew daisies and, by the looks of his raised planter in the back, lots of other things.

Tomato plants were tied neatly to stakes. Tiny mounds of lettuce filled an entire row. Carrot stems peeked from the rich-looking soil, as did rows and rows of other vegetables. Her focus turned from his garden to her yard, which was such a mess. The only thing growing were weeds. She wiped her hand on a towel and turned to Kellyn, who sat waiting for her breakfast.

"How about we work in the yard today?"

Kellyn took a bite and smiled. Marina wasn't sure if it was the chocolate or the fact that they would play in the dirt together that made her happy, but she'd take whatever she could get. While her daughter never spoke, she also rarely smiled, so this was a moment to take in and remember.

"I thought we could plant a garden like Sheriff Cooper." Marina lifted in her chair to take another glance next door. The water and the man were gone, but the green garden remained, and somehow it became a symbol of hope.

If a garden could sprout from mountain soil where the air was thin and arid, then she and Kellyn could plant roots and thrive. With new-found energy, she waited for her daughter to finish her breakfast while she planted rows of vegetables in her mind.

Marina didn't have much, but they walked into the overgrown yard with kitchen shears and a metal spoon. She'd started with less and survived.

They began in the right corner. It was grass-free and contained the remnants of a long-lost garden. While she tugged at the brambles and weeds, Kellyn dug in the ground with the kitchen spoon.

"It will take you years to till the soil that way." A deep voice sounded from behind her. Marina leaped into the air and swung around with her fists pulled up and the scissors ready to strike. When she saw it was Sheriff Cooper, she let them fall to her side.

He raised his hands in surrender, though he never let go of the hoe and shovel. "I come in peace."

Marina looked at Kellyn, who had moved far away. Her knuckles had turned white with the force of her grip. "Hang on one second." She walked over to her baby girl and squatted in front of her. "You're okay. I'm okay. It's okay. He's being neighborly. You can stay here and help, or you can go inside and read Mrs. Beasley a story. It's up to you." She returned to the sheriff, who had moved to her plot of land.

He turned the soil like it was nothing. "Gardening is more effective if you have the right tools."

She glanced at the kitchen shears in her hand and laughed. "You don't think these will work?" She realized she'd been gripping them like a weapon.

"Sure, if you're going to shank the ground or give the weeds a trim." He swiped the sweat from his brow.

She took in his appearance for the first time. He was a good-looking man. Her mom used to tell her that a man's soul was found in his eyes. The sheriff had kind brown eyes. The sunlight danced off the amber specs, making it look like they were dipped in gold. She should have thought about eyes when she met Craig. His were dark, like caves of nothingness. That should have been her first clue.

"I could give it a cut, that's what I do, but I fear I'd have a hard time getting a return on my investment of time and talent."

He moved with ease across the land, digging and turning the soil while Marina followed to loosen the dead plants. "While I appreciate your help, Sheriff Cooper, I don't want to take up any more of your day."

He stopped and put one boot on the shovel, cupped the handle, and laid his chin on top. "I've found few things grow without care—not a garden and not friendship. Anything worth having is worth cultivating. We're neighbors, Marina, and I'd like to be friends." He lifted his head and pressed his foot on the shovel again. "Call me Aiden."

The man in front of her was sexy, kind, and considerate—that made him dangerous. But he also had a shovel and a hoe which made him a valuable asset for a woman who wanted a garden.

"I appreciate the help, Aiden. I have little to offer you right now, but I'll share my harvest if I can get anything to grow."

He smiled and continued to till the soil. "All this needs is attention, water, and some tender loving care." He pulled several packets from his pocket. "And maybe some seeds."

She'd never felt so giddy over a few packets of seeds. She took them from his hand and saw there was everything to make a salad from lettuce to tomatoes. "I can replace these."

"They're a gift." He looked at Kellyn. "Do you think she'd like to help us plant them when we're done?"

Marina felt awful that she hadn't introduced

Kellyn to him, but she also didn't want to push her. She was apprehensive around strangers, especially men.

"Kellyn, honey, come over here and meet Sher... Mr. Cooper."

"Mr. Cooper was my father." Aiden laughed. "Way to make a guy feel old."

Kellyn lifted her head and watched him with a wary eye. She looked at Marina and then back at the ground she'd dug with her spoon. She took a long minute before she dropped the spoon and crept to Marina, taking her place behind her legs. She fisted Marina's pants and peeked around the side to where Aiden stood.

He dropped to his knees, making Kellyn pull back.

"She's shy. She doesn't speak, but she understands you."

Most men didn't have time for a little girl who was more of a shadow than a presence, but Aiden smiled. "Hello, Kellyn. I love your name. I think we should plant a flower and name it after you. What do you think?"

Marina stepped to the side so he could see her daughter. "She loves daisies."

"Is that right?" Aiden walked to the chain-link fence. Its four-foot height didn't stop him from reaching over and picking several of the flowers from his garden. He returned and showed the daisies to Kellyn. "How about a flower for every year you've lived?" He plucked one from the small bouquet and offered it to her. She took it and stared at the rest in his hand. "Oh, you're older than one. Right." He passed another and another and looked at her. "How many more do I owe you?"

To Marina's surprise, Kellyn held up a single finger, and Aiden placed the fourth flower in her tiny little palm. She looked up at Marina and down at the flowers.

"She's almost five."

"Wow, such a big girl. Do you think your mom should have one for every year she's lived too?"

An almost imperceptible nod moved her head.

"Oh no," Marina said. "That would strip your garden bare."

"I doubt that."

Kellyn took her flowers back to the spot where she'd dug a hole and planted the stems into the ground.

"Oh, honey, they won—" Marina started to say they wouldn't grow, but Aiden stopped her.

"Let her plant them. You never know what might happen." He returned to digging the soil.

"She's lived with enough disappointment in her life, I hate to add to it." She could see the gears in Aiden's head move and knew she'd said too much.

"Tell me about you two and what brings you to Aspen Cove."

Yep, she'd said too much. She wanted as few people to know about her life as possible. How was she supposed to start over if she had to go back to the beginning all the time? "Not much to tell. We wanted a change. I've always found Aspen Cove to be a place of comfort, so when the opportunity came for us to move, I chose to relocate here. Tell me about your garden." The subject change was abrupt but needed.

Aiden continued to dig while she removed the debris and garbage. "I love that I can plant a seed and start something wonderful. Like anything, you get out of it what you put into it." He glanced at the space that took half his yard. "I started with tomatoes and carrots a few years ago. Now I grow everything from eggplant to pumpkins." Pride showed in his smile. "This year I'll try to outgrow last year's biggest pumpkin, which was over a hundred pounds."

Marina stopped and stared. "You grew a hundred-pound pumpkin?"

"Yep."

"Why?"

"Why not? Maybe Kellyn can grow a pumpkin this year too."

At the mention of her name, she looked up from

planting her flowers, which had already started to wilt. She gave them a look and walked inside the house.

"Maybe. She's—"

"She's lovely. I don't know what she's been through, but I can see you're the perfect mother for her. You water and care for her like she's a delicate flower. She will grow, and she will flourish." He bent over and picked up the seed packets they'd left on the ground. "She's like a seedling waiting to take root."

It surprised Marina that Aiden saw all that in the short time he'd spent with her. Marina always felt Kellyn would be okay, eventually. Although her natural family treated her like a weed, Marina knew she'd grow up as pretty as a flower and as strong as an oak tree. All she needed was love and care.

"I should check on her."

Aiden leaned the shovel and hoe against the fence. "Thanks for spending your morning with me. It's been nice." He pointed to the small building near the back of his house. "Feel free to borrow anything you need. The shed is always open. I'll leave these here for you in case you want to work on it more."

She shook her head and wiped the perspiration from her forehead. "I think I'm done for the day. It's hot, and I still have a lot of unpacking to do."

"Fair enough." He gathered his tools and walked out her gate and into his yard. "I'm here if you need me for anything."

Was it possible for a man to be so nice? She liked to believe she was a good judge of character, but that hadn't been true with her ex. Then again, she'd fallen in love with his daughter, not him. Somehow being so wrong about a man made something so right in her life.

When she entered the house, she found Kellyn sitting on the Formica counter and staring out the window. She followed her line of sight straight to Aiden, who was back to working in his garden.

"He seems like a nice man." Marina leaned forward to watch him pluck the weeds from between the rows of vegetables.

Kellyn climbed down and walked away.

CHAPTER FOUR

Aiden changed into his uniform and went to the office to check on his deputy. Mark wouldn't be feeling up to par after having a quick bout of the stomach flu, but he had a rare work ethic for a young man and wouldn't take off more time than absolutely necessary.

Today Aiden was happy to come in late. It gave him a chance to get to know Marina better.

"Look who finally came to work." Mark shifted from the big desk in the center of the room to the smaller one in the corner. "Word has it you were tilling the soil with the hottie next door."

"You're worse than an old lady."

Mark threw his hands up. "What? I'm just telling you what I heard."

Aiden went to the coffeepot that was always full no matter what time of day he came in. He had Poppy Dawson to thank for that. She made sure they were continuously loaded with fully leaded coffee and muffins. "Poppy been in today?" While she only pulled a few shifts a week, she checked in frequently. Something told Aiden it had more to do with his young deputy than her love of the job or her need to make coffee.

"She stopped by earlier." By the blush on Mark's face, Aiden knew he was right to assume there was something going on between them.

"Don't let her father catch you trying to till her soil. He's got a collection of rifles that would rival any hunter's. Besides, I hear he's a crack shot."

"Whatever. There's nothing going on." Mark shook his head. "She's not my type."

Aiden laughed. "Why, because she bathes and smells pretty?"

Mark frowned. "No, because she's..." He got all flustered and plopped into the seat in front of him. "Oh hell, because she's way too good for me."

Aiden took his coffee to his desk and sat on the edge, looking at the young man in front of him. He'd only known Mark a few years, but he was a good kid. Raised by a single mother, he'd no doubt missed out on the fatherly advice every young man should receive.

Aiden took a sip of coffee and set the cup on his desk. "My father always told me to find a woman I didn't deserve and then rise to the occasion to make myself worthy of her."

Mark looked out the window like he was looking for Poppy. "I want to be that man, but look at me. I'm a deputy sheriff. I make just above the poverty level, and I've got nothing to offer her."

Aiden hated sounding like a damn chick flick, but the message seemed right. "Offer her your heart. That's all most women want."

He seemed to chew on that for a few minutes. "What about you, Coop? You going to hook up with the divorcée?"

"Who?" He played stupid.

Mark leaned back in his chair. "Marina. Word on the street is she's recently divorced. Bad marriage and all. Took the kid and ran."

"Ran?" That sounded awful. Sounded dangerous, but with how skittish she was added to the fear that clouded her daughter's eyes, it sounded about right. "Is she in danger?"

"Not sure." He opened his drawer and took out a piece of paper that had the name Marina Caswell at the top right under the words "restraining order."

Aiden took the page from his hands and stared at the name. "Holy shit, she's a Caswell." That changed a lot of things. He wondered if he should reach out to Chief Caswell in Copper Creek. He didn't much care for the man, with all his boastfulness and blunder. He was kind of like a comic strip cop on steroids. "How'd you get this?"

Mark looked at the ceiling as if the answer would come from above. "Well, seeing as you were her neighbor and all, I figured you'd want to know as much about her as possible." He opened his drawer again and pulled out a file on Marina. "I ran a check on her."

"You what?" It wasn't like Aiden hadn't wanted to do the same. He had, but he was trying to do the right thing. "You overstepped your boundaries. You can't run a check on someone just because." He held out his hand. "Give me that." As Mark was about to give it to him, Aiden dropped his hand. "No...put it in the shred pile. We will not be using city resources to spy on our neighbors."

Mark rose and placed the folder on top of the shred pile. "Just trying to help, boss."

"You want to help? Go over to the diner and get us both the special." He took out his wallet and pulled out a twenty to hand to Mark.

He waited until Mark rounded the corner to grab the folder from the pile. There was no use wasting good information. If confronted about it, he could honestly say he hadn't asked for the details. They had simply shown up.

He took another glance out the window to make sure he wouldn't get his hand caught in the proverbial cookie jar. The first page was simple information. Marina Caswell was thirty. She'd been married once to Craig Caswell, who ran the Copper Creek Zoning Commission. His father was the mayor of Copper Creek. His brother was the DA for the town. Nothing happened in Copper Creek unless it passed the desk of a Caswell.

He lifted the restraining order to see who it was filed against. He dropped it when he saw the name Craig Caswell and the reason being domestic violence.

Nothing made him angrier than a cowardly man. In his mind, only a coward would hit a woman or a child. That she could get a restraining order said something about the extent of the problem. There was no way the Caswells would have allowed it to be filed if she didn't have something major on them.

He was bent over picking up the paper when the bell on the door rang. The smell of fried chicken wafted through the air, meaning Mark was back with lunch. Not wanting to be caught snooping, Aiden gathered the pages and shoved them into his side drawer. He rushed from his seat to take the container Mark offered.

The young deputy looked to the shred pile and

smiled. "You sure you don't want to look through the information I compiled?"

Aiden picked up the buttermilk biscuit from his to-go box and flung it at Mark's head. "Are you sure you want to stay employed?"

Mark brushed the crumbs from his tan shirt and laughed. "She really is pretty," he said before he shoved the broken biscuit into his mouth.

"You better be talking about Poppy Dawson, young man. You might have a chance with her if you learn to use utensils and chew your food." The two men sat in silence. By the look on Mark's face, he was thinking about Poppy. He had that soft look all men got when they had a crush on a girl. Well... all men before they found their girl in bed with someone else. From that point on, their look was tinged with distrust. He knew that look well. He wore it like a badge and had seen it on Marina's face both times he approached her.

He finished his meal and picked up his keys. "I'm heading out. I'll check in later. I've got some stuff to take care of in Copper Creek."

Mark's eyes grew wide. "You're not visiting the Caswells, are you?"

While that sounded like a good plan, it wasn't his. "Nope. I've got more tilling of the soil to do, and I need supplies. Besides, I had to pull a double yesterday, so you owe me." Aiden held up his cell phone. "Call if you need anything."

———

HE HADN'T FELT like this in years. Adrenaline rushed through his veins as he snuck into Marina's yard well after midnight.

Was this how his friends Wes and Lydia felt when they were lurking around the neighborhood to TP trees and steal yard gnomes? He'd been their first victim, but not their last. He had to give them credit because they'd taken shenanigans to a whole new level. Who thought vandalism and theft could be a good thing, but it was because they'd held people's yard art as hostages and traded them for favors and donations to those less fortunate.

As Aiden snuck into Marina and Kellyn's backyard with his shovel and hoe, all he had in mind was putting a smile on both their faces. He'd raided the outdoor store in Copper Creek and bought all the plants he could fit in the back of his cruiser. While seeds were good, high altitude gardening was a different beast. The growing season was far too short to start this late. The only way they would see the fruits of their labor was to start with seedlings.

He'd waited for the lights to go off in the house

before he began the arduous task of planting their garden by moonlight.

His first job was to create a space just for Kellyn. She'd already picked out her plot and started digging with a kitchen spoon. It was adorable the way she'd buried the stems of the daisies he'd given her as if they would magically grow. While he was at the garden center, he thought, *Why not bring her a little magic?* There was no reason those flowers couldn't grow overnight, so he bought several varieties of daisies and planted them in the exact place Kellyn had stuck her wilted stems.

Once that was taken care of, he went to work on the rest. Hours later, he stood back and looked at his accomplishments. His back ached, and the beginning of blisters rose on his hands, but he'd never felt better.

He'd broken the law. He'd trespassed. He'd altered private property. He'd turned neglected, fallow land into something wonderful, and he'd do it again if it brought a smile to Marina's and Kellyn's faces.

He had no idea why it mattered so much to him. Could be that he was bored. Might be he was lonely. Most likely it was because Marina Caswell and her daughter intrigued him.

He showered and climbed into bed, feeling like

he'd moved mountains when in reality, it was just a few wheelbarrows of dirt.

He thought about his father before he closed his eyes. How lucky was he to have such a good role model? By the time Aiden was ten, he knew his father's requirements for being a good man.

Be honorable.

Be a gentleman.

Admit when you're wrong.

Have an opinion, but respect others' rights to have one as well.

Know when to fight and when to back down.

Know how to complete a task. Deviate by choice, not by ignorance.

Take care of yourself and your property.

Stand up for those who can't stand up for themselves.

Always strive to be a better man.

You're only as good as the woman standing beside you. Choose your mate wisely.

That was his one failure so far. Next time he fell in love, he'd be smarter. He needed to find a woman willing to treat a relationship like a garden. She needed to be willing to till the soil, to plant seeds of opportunity and love, and to water the friendship and watch it grow into more.

Marina's face came to mind. Could she be the one?

CHAPTER FIVE

Marina stood at the kitchen sink with her mouth wide open. She rubbed her eyes to make sure she wasn't seeing things. She even leaned forward until the window hit her forehead, certain she'd been sleepwalking or dreaming. When her face touched the sun-warmed glass, she knew it was real.

Perfect rows of fruits and vegetables reached for the early morning sunshine. She scanned the garden and knew without a doubt she'd been given the greatest gift.

"Kellyn," she called. "Sweetie. Come here."

Dragging Mrs. Beasley by the arm, Kellyn padded into the kitchen wearing her pink popsicle pajamas and a look of confusion.

Marina swept her off her feet and hugged her

to her chest. "Look." She pointed out the window at the newly planted garden. "Look at your daisies. They grew." Her daughter's eyes opened wide with surprise. "Get dressed. We need to go look."

The only time Kellyn moved quickly was when she was running from something, so to see her leave her precious doll in the center of the floor and race to her room made Marina's heart swell with joy.

She was back in less than a minute, wearing a mismatch of colors. No one could tell her that plaid shorts weren't the perfect match for her polka-dotted shirt. It didn't matter that she had two different colored socks on or her shoes were on the wrong feet, Kellyn was ready to conquer this day, and she was doing it with a smile.

They stepped out the back door and raced to the garden.

Off to her right, Marina saw movement. She turned to see Aiden Cooper lean against the fence. The damn man wasn't even dressed. All he wore was a pair of low-slung sweatpants. His chest was bare, as were his feet. She wasn't sure which was a more beautiful sight—the tiny little plants in her garden or the broad-chested man standing so close she could almost reach out and touch the dusting of hair that led to a trail disappearing beneath his elastic waistband.

"Can I look at your garden?" His smile was almost as broad as his chest.

"Yes, come on over." Marina stepped to where Kellyn leaned over to smell her daisies. "You wouldn't happen to know a garden fairy, would you?"

Aiden hoisted himself over the four-foot fence with ease. "No, I'm as surprised as you." His eyes danced with delight. "It must be Kellyn who brought the magic with her."

Kellyn glanced up from her flowers with a look of wonder and awe. Marina hadn't seen that look on her face—ever.

"Hey, Kellyn, how did you get your flowers to grow so fast?" Aiden asked. "Did you sprinkle magic dust on them?"

Her sweet daughter stared at the flowers and then looked at Aiden before she shook her head. That she acknowledged his question was huge. She didn't respond to many people and never to men.

"They're beautiful, just like you and your mommy."

Marina didn't feel beautiful. She felt rough and worn out like she'd lived a thousand years in the past two. She brushed her fingers through her hair, having forgotten that she'd also just gotten out of bed. To her horror, she felt the knots give as she combed through the mess.

Dressed in sleep shorts and a tank, she was at least decent but nowhere near beautiful. She couldn't remember the last time she'd felt remotely pretty.

"I'm a wreck," she said.

"I think you look lovely." He took her in from her messy hair to her dime-store rubber flip-flops.

His eyes had dark circles under them, but there was no hint of deception. "You look like you've been up all night gardening," she whispered, so she wouldn't spoil the magic for Kellyn. She couldn't help the smile that stretched her lips. No one had ever done anything so kind for her.

"Me? Nope, I leave the midnight gardening to the fairies."

Marina glanced at the garden and back at Aiden. It must have taken him hours to plant everything, and the money he'd spent made her heart race.

"This is maybe the best thing that's ever happened to us." She leaned over and brushed her fingers across the strawberry plant leaves. It was too much for a stranger to give. "I don't have a lot of money." It was embarrassing for her to admit she had nothing. "I can try to pay you back over time."

She watched his brow furrow and his lips stretch thin. While she hated her unconscious reaction to step back, she knew it would take time to re-train herself.

"Like I said, I don't know who your fairy is, but I'm pleased that you're happy with the work."

She turned back to the garden. Kellyn had plucked a purple daisy from her new plant and walked toward her. Marina held out her hand, expecting her daughter to give her a flower. Only she didn't. Kellyn walked past Marina and handed the flower to Aiden.

"Oh my God, you don't understand what a gift that is."

Aiden squatted down, so he was eye to eye with Kellyn. "Thank you, beautiful. I've never had anyone give me a flower before. This is so special." He moved forward to pat her head, but she dashed out of his reach.

Aiden's smile faltered for a second but was back in place when he stood. "I just made a fresh pot of coffee. Would you like a cup?"

While Marina wanted to say yes, she'd already promised Kellyn another trip to the bakery. "Can I have a rain check? We have a date with a cranberry orange muffin."

Aiden nodded and jumped back over the fence. "I can't compete with that."

Marina laughed. "You just did." She risked everything to lean over and give him a quick hug. It was a simple gesture, but one that made her heart beat fast and hard. "Thanks for making us feel welcome." She looked over her shoulder at everything he'd done. "I'm going to be the best gardener on the block."

He laughed. "Hey now, don't make me call the garden fairies over to get rid of the competition."

She laughed. It felt wonderful to really laugh. "Okay, I'll settle for second best."

He leaned forward and whispered, "No, don't you ever settle for less again. You deserve more." He turned and walked away.

She stood there for a few minutes, wondering what he knew about her. Kellyn tugged on her hand and gave the sign that she was hungry. She might not speak, but that didn't mean she couldn't communicate.

THEY ARRIVED at the bakery to find Katie looking frazzled. She jostled an unhappy baby in her hands while she tried to fill the display case.

Marina sat Kellyn at a nearby table and rushed to help. "You want me to take the baby or fill the display case?"

Katie looked at her fussy baby and smiled. "I could use a minute break." She passed Sahara off to

Marina and plated up a few muffins. "She's teething, and I swear she waits until she's with me to get cranky." Katie came around the counter to where Marina sat bouncing Sahara on her lap, and Kellyn took out her crayons and coloring book. "She was a perfect angel for Bowie." Her daughter reached for Kellyn's hair and happily cooed. "Traitor."

"You're not a traitor, are you? You just wanted some variety." A string of drool dripped from the baby's mouth to Marina's T-shirt.

"You'll be a mess when you leave." Katie took a napkin from the holder and wiped Sahara's chin, which only made her fuss louder. "I give up."

"Do you ever get a break?"

"Sure, my friend Sage will take her from time to time, and my in-laws Maisey and Ben are amazing, but the days are tough, especially when the sitter calls in sick like today. I don't like to have her in the bakery so close to the ovens and mixer. It's not a safe place for a baby."

Sahara fussed until Marina turned her around to face Kellyn. They seemed to connect in some odd silent way. Both little girls reached out to each other and touched fingers. Sahara squealed with delight.

"Where's your husband?" She'd noticed the Bait and Tackle Shop was closed for the day.

"He went to Silver Springs to pick up supplies. Big fishing season, and he was out of bait. Not good for the only bait shop within miles."

The timer on the oven went off, and Katie rushed to take the brownies out while Marina picked at the muffins she had brought them.

"Chocolate milk?" Katie called to Kellyn over the counter.

Remarkably, Kellyn nodded. While Marina had worried that staying this close to Copper Creek was a risk because it put her and Kellyn within reach of Craig, it might have been a good move after all. In just a few days, Kellyn had relaxed and let her guard down.

"We aren't doing much this afternoon. I know you don't know me well, but I can take her home with me, and you can pick her up after the bakery closes." Marina looked at how well Kellyn and Sahara were getting on. They seemed spellbound by one another. "It would help me too because Kellyn seems enamored with your little sprite."

Katie chewed on her lip for a second. "That would be great. I've got a huge muffin order to make, and I had no idea how I would get it done."

"It's a deal then."

"A deal if you let me pay you. I would pay for the sitter, anyway."

While Marina could use the money, she shook

her head. "You already paid me with your friendship."

Katie rushed behind the counter to do more stocking. "My friendship is free as well as those muffins. You're a godsend."

Marina waited for Kellyn to finish her chocolate milk and muffin before they got Sahara's car seat and diaper bag and went home. She put a soft comforter in the center of the living room floor and placed little Sahara on top. Kellyn took her place beside the baby.

She watched her daughter look after the Sahara as if she was hers. She even let her give her a bottle when the baby seemed to tire. An hour later, both girls were lying side by side, sound asleep.

Would she ever have the chance to have a baby of her own? She never felt as if Kellyn wasn't hers. She'd taken over full-time mothering from the moment they met, but she wondered what it would feel like to have the child of a man she loved growing inside her. To feel it move with a life force created by two people in love.

She was caught up in her daydream when a soft knock sounded from the door. On the doorstep, she found a tired but content-looking Katie. In her hands was a bakery box filled with muffins.

She led her into the kitchen where she made her a cup of tea.

"Wow," Katie said, looking out the window. "You've been busy."

Marina could feel the heat of her blush. "No, it would seem that I moved next door to the garden fairy."

"Aiden planted your garden?"

Marina shrugged. "It would seem so. He's not confessing, but he's the only one who could have done it. The question is, why?" She'd pondered that question while the girls took their naps. In fact, Aiden Cooper had consumed much of her thoughts the entire day.

"He's not the kind of man to have a motive. He's just a good man."

"I've not met many of them." She took two cups of tea into the living room so they could keep an eye on the girls in case they stirred.

"There are more good ones out there than people would make you believe." Katie sipped her tea and hummed. "I also feel like you have to challenge men to be better."

It took everything for Marina not to choke on her tea. "Challenging my ex brought me a lot of trouble."

Katie pointed toward Aiden's house. "He's not your ex. Don't make him pay the price for that," she whispered, "asshole's sins."

"You're right." She was right. It was part of Marina's new not-a-victim-but-a-victor mantra. Everyone deserved a chance. Innocent until proven otherwise.

"Looks like you're getting all settled in."

There wasn't much in her house. She and Kellyn had the basics, but she'd get more when she could. "It's a work in progress. I'll fix it up." While the place was in good shape, the paint had yellowed, and the floor had dulled, but it was a roof over their heads. "Know anyone who can use a haircut, perm, or color? I'll need to find work soon if we're going to stay. While this place is great, it comes with rent, utilities, and maintenance costs."

Katie laughed. "And a fairy garden."

"Yes, there is that."

"So...about Aiden. Do you think he's cute?"

CHAPTER SIX

"Do you think she's cute?" Wes asked as Aiden followed him around The Guild Creative Center. Because the building had once belonged to his ancestors, it was Wes's pride and joy. He loved to show it off to anyone who would take the time for a tour. They walked inside the building that would eventually house artists of every type. Only weeks ago, it was drywall and sawdust, but today it looked more like a museum waiting for a masterpiece.

Aiden made it a point to show up all over town, especially since there was an influx of workers moving to Aspen Cove. More importantly, he loved to support his friends that were making a difference.

"Do I think who's cute?" He knew exactly who Wes referred to. Hell, the whole town had Marina and him walking down the aisle already, and she'd been here less than a week. Planting her garden had been the right thing to do, but it sure got tongues wagging.

"Marina Caswell, you idiot."

"She's easy on the eyes." Marina Caswell was gorgeous with her long brown hair and eyes the color of a clear summer sky.

"So, you like her?"

Aiden ignored the question and walked into what used to be a wide-open warehouse. "When will this be done?"

Wes walked ahead of him. "Good deflection, but we're coming back to the subject of your neighbor in a second." He showed Aiden where Samantha's recording studio was located, which was right next door to Dalton's culinary school. Abby, the local beekeeper, had already reserved a space for the products she produced from her bee-hives. She sold everything from honey to candles.

Wes pointed out the dozen or so studios avail-able for artists of all types. He had a secret wish list of potential clients from painters to sculptors to his favorite, a stationery maker.

"It would be so great if she takes the place. To have a woman who makes stationery from pulp is like going back to the beginning." The Guild Cre-ative Center used to be The Guild Paper Factory in its heyday until they closed years ago and killed the growth of the town.

Bringing it full circle felt right. Reliving a piece of his past and preserving it for the future was important to Wes. The town could not have chosen a better project manager, but Aiden imagined he'd be a bit nostalgic for a time when there was less traffic, although he knew all things required change to prosper. This brought his thoughts to his neighbor.

"Do you know Marina?"

They walked outside where Wes had a cooler filled with water and sports drinks. He offered one to Aiden, and they took a seat at the picnic table in the shade.

"Know her? No. But I owe her a great deal." He turned to look at the building. "None of this would be possible if she hadn't shown up in the permits department the day I went there to get the final permits signed. Her husband—"

"Ex-husband," Aiden blurted. He didn't know why it was so critical to clarify, but it was important for him to get it right.

"Yes, Craig Caswell was sitting at his desk, acting like he owned the world. He'd been delaying our permits for both the fire station and The Guild Creative Center for weeks. It's like his family doesn't want to see Aspen Cove grow." He shook his head. "Anyway...I was in the office when she arrived. Craig was put out that she was interrupting his day. She marched in like a sacrifice to the slaughter and slammed a flash drive on his desk. She said something about his father being really interested before she walked out."

"No shit?" Aiden sat up taller. He wished he could have seen that moment—been a fly on the wall. He loved it when anyone came into their power and realized they had control over their lives. Had that been the pinnacle moment for Marina? The day she decided her marriage to Craig Caswell was over?

"She told him to sign the permits. Made it sound like he had bigger problems, and he surprised the hell out of me by signing off on them. I swiped the papers from his desk and took off before he could change his mind."

Aiden knew that Craig Caswell had abused his wife and most likely his daughter. He'd seen the restraining order dated several weeks back. The timing was too close to have been coincidental.

"She seems like a nice woman, and her little girl is darling." He still had the daisy she'd pressed into his hand. It didn't take Marina telling him what a big deal that was. He'd seen how apprehensive she was—how withdrawn. It bothered him that Kellyn could physically talk but chose not to. Something had silenced her. A chill ran up his spine thinking about how awful that something had to be to steal her words forever.

"What are you going to do about her?" Wes finished his water and tossed the plastic bottle into a nearby trash can.

"Kellyn?" He had no plans to do anything about anyone.

"No, your attraction to Marina."

"Who says I'm attracted to her?"

"You didn't say you weren't."

Aiden rose from the bench and started toward his cruiser. "Look, man, she's nice. She's pretty. She smells good." Like coconut cream pie. "She also has a lot of baggage, and she doesn't come across as a woman looking for anything but space. Definitely not a woman looking for a man."

They got to the cruiser, and Wes leaned into the door. "We've all got baggage. Most of us think we want space, but the reality is we want someone to share our space." He pushed off the SUV and walked away.

Aiden climbed into his vehicle and sat there for a minute, thinking about what Wes had said. There was probably some truth to his words, but if Marina didn't want space, what did she want? The word *friendship* came to mind.

He immediately drove to the diner and ordered a family meal of fried chicken with all the fixings. If

Marina didn't want to join him on a picnic, he'd at least have food for the rest of the week.

After he stopped by the office to tell Mark he was calling it a day, he headed back home. He was relieved to see her car in the driveway, but his heart raced at the thought of asking her out.

While he changed into shorts and a T-shirt, he reminded himself that it wasn't a date. He was simply offering his friendship. Surely two friends could enjoy a picnic at the park together. Also, Kellyn needed to explore her new surroundings, and what better place to do that than at a place with swings, slides, and other children?

He wiped his sweaty palms on his shorts and knocked on her door. He hadn't been this nervous since he'd asked Cindy Masters to the prom.

Her footsteps approached the door. A shadow crossed the peephole, and then there was a delay. *Is she debating on whether to answer the door?* He heard the chain drop first, followed by the deadbolt.

"Aiden." The way she said his name in that breathy feminine voice made his chest tighten.

"Hey, Marina." He stood there like a deer in the headlights, trying to figure out what to say. He was rusty when it came to women, and he didn't know how to approach the subject. He figured he might as well just lay it out for what it was, a simple invite to have dinner. "I know it's last minute, and you and Kellyn might have dinner plans, but I was hoping I could convince you to join me on a picnic at Hope Park."

Behind Marina stood Kellyn with her blue polka-dotted doll in her hands. While her body was facing him, her feet were awkwardly placed in the opposite direction as if ready to run.

"Oh...umm...we..."

He knew she was trying to come up with a reason to say no, so he pleaded his case. "Please don't make me eat fried chicken for the rest of the week."

Marina smiled, and even though it was a barely there lift to her lips, it filled Aiden with so much happiness.

"It's just a picnic. Besides, I thought Kellyn might enjoy the playground, and if we're lucky, there will be other children there for her to play with."

Marina looked over her shoulder at her daughter. "Are you up for a push on the swings?" Kellyn nodded and tossed her doll to the sofa.

Marina giggled. "I guess that's a yes."

Relief swept through Aiden. "Perfect. I'll wait by my car."

Marina looked at the police cruiser. "We're taking your work car?"

He shook his head, "Nope, I have other transportation. Can I grab her booster seat?"

Marina twisted her lips in thought. "How about we follow you?"

He reminded himself that she didn't really know him. He was happy she was being cautious, and he was determined to earn her trust. "All right, I'll meet you there."

He transferred the food from his cruiser to his car. While he would have liked to show off his pride and joy, he'd have to wait for another day to give them a ride in his Mustang convertible.

He beat them to the park and had a blanket laid out and the food on display when they pulled up. Marina looked cautiously around before she took Kellyn out of the back seat of her SUV.

Aiden smiled as they walked hand in hand toward him. He dropped to his knees on the blanket and looked at Kellyn, who always stood behind Marina's legs.

"Are you hungry?"

She said nothing as she moved to the far side of the blanket and pulled three colored pieces of wood from her bag. She set the red, yellow, and green cylinders next to her and waited. After a minute, she pushed the green one forward.

"She feels safe with you."

A heated squeeze grabbed Aiden's heart. "I'm

glad." He busied himself handing out plates and unwrapping containers of chicken, potato salad, and baked beans.

Marina took a bite and hummed. "I can't remember the last time we did something like this. Far too long ago for sure."

Aiden had forgotten about the drinks and reached into the only unopened bag to get the cans of punch he'd picked up at The Corner Store. He'd stood there staring at the drinks for minutes until the owner, Marge, asked him what the problem was. He explained that he didn't know what a four-year-old liked. She handed him a six-pack of fruit punch and told him he couldn't go wrong with sugar and red dye. Two things all kids seemed to love.

He popped the top and handed it to Kellyn. She didn't get a good grip on it before he let go, and the can tumbled over, spilling red liquid on her shirt and the blanket below. She went from happy to terrified in a second. Her face turned ashen white, and silent tears ran from her eyes. She scrambled away and grabbed for the red cylinder.

Marina's face took on a look of fear he'd never seen a grown woman show, but she shuttered it quickly and grabbed a few napkins. "Kellyn, it's okay," she soothed. She looked at Aiden as if checking to make sure her words were true.

Aiden didn't know what to do, so he picked up the half-empty can of fruit punch and dumped it on his shirt. "I love that color on you," he said to Kellyn. "What do you think? Can I wear it too?" His powder-blue shirt soaked up the liquid and turned a muted shade of purple.

Kellyn peeked around her mom and saw what he'd done. Her little head tilted in confusion. Even Marina gave him a strange look.

"It's only spilled punch. It's not a big deal."

Marina grabbed a few more napkins and offered them to him to blot the liquid from his shirt. "That will stain."

Aiden chuckled. "Perfect. I hear I look good in red." He looked down at his shirt. "And purple." He pulled a new can of punch from the bag and offered it to Kellyn. She stared at it for a long minute. It was as if she thought he might trick her. "This time, I'll let you open it. I'm so sorry I spilled the punch on you, but you look good in the color too."

For a minute, he thought she'd bury herself behind Marina again, but to his surprise, she took her seat and the punch. Next, she dropped the red cylinder and picked up the yellow one. His heart broke for her. *What the hell had happened to them?*

The rest of the meal was eaten in relative silence until Louise and Bobby Williams showed up with their seven children. Kellyn watched the kids play on the swings, the slide, and the merry-go-round.

"Is it okay if she plays?"

Marina glanced at the big family having fun. "Sure, but she won't go. She rarely leaves my side."

Another heartbreaking truth, but then something miraculous happened. Kellyn stood and walked toward the swings.

When she was out of earshot. Marina choked back a cry. "I don't believe it."

They sat on the edge of the blanket and stared at Kellyn as she took the only open swing. She was too small to touch the ground once she hopped up, so she sat there, dangling and swinging her feet back and forth.

Aiden handed Marina the last dry napkin and helped her stand. "I don't know what your history is, but I'm glad you're here, and I'll do whatever I can to help."

She gave him a half smile. "You've been kind to us. We aren't used to that."

He wrapped his arm around her shoulders. At first, she stiffened but then relaxed. "Shall we go play with your daughter?"

Her pace picked up as they neared the swing set. "Yes, she loves to swing."

Aiden stood back and watched while Marina pulled Kellyn back and pushed her forward again and again. When she finished, one of the Williams girls came over and took Kellyn's hand, leading her to the sandbox.

He walked Marina back to the blanket. "I'm a great listener if you ever want to talk."

She reached over and patted his hand. "Thank you. If I started talking, I may never shut up."

Aiden cleaned up the dinner mess and took a seat beside her. "That's fine. I like your voice."

She rolled her upper lip between her teeth and let it pop loose. "I'm not sure what you're looking for, but I have to be honest. I need a man in my life like I need another black eye."

He internally winced. "I'm sorry you've been through that experience." She'd confirmed what he already knew. When he worked in Colorado Springs, he'd seen his share of domestic abuse victims. "I'm not that man. It looks like you can use a friend."

"I really can," she said in an almost whisper.

An orange glow blanketed them as the sun began to set. Kellyn came back to them as soon as the Williams children gathered around their parents to leave.

Aiden called the family over to introduce them to Marina. Bobby Williams owned the only gas station and car repair shop in town. His wife Louise was pregnant with their eighth child. Rather than offer a handshake, Louise pulled Marina in for a bear hug. "So glad to have you and your little girl in the neighborhood." She let Marina go and ruffled Kellyn's hair. "Your daughter is sweet. If you ever need a break, bring her by the house. We have so many kids we'd hardly notice one more."

Once the Williamses were out of sight, Aiden packed up the blanket and led the girls to their car. While the afternoon had started off on the shaky side, he felt good about how it ended.

Rather than walk on her mother's far side, Kellyn took up the space between him and Marina. Another win for him.

When they got to the car, she moved her little hand from her lips outward.

"She says thank you."

Did he dare try to touch her? He would have loved to be able to pull the little thing in for a hug, but he didn't want to send her searching for her red wooden cylinder again. Instead, he smiled and touched her nose with his finger.

"Thanks for the best night I've had in a long time."

He moved back as she climbed into her booster seat. Marina stood in front of him. He offered her his hand to shake, but she surprised him when she leaned in and gave him a tentative hug. Her lips lifted to a sly smile when she stepped back and looked at his stained shirt. "You do look good in red."

His brows lifted. "How good?"

She made sure Kellyn was buckled in before she closed the door. "Too good." She climbed into her seat and shut the door, but before it closed all the way, Aiden was certain he heard her say, "You're going to be trouble for me."

He laughed all the way to his car. *Oh, sweetheart, you're already trouble.*

CHAPTER SEVEN

Marina woke with a smile on her face and lightness in her chest that she hadn't felt for two years. She sat on the back steps and watched Kellyn water the garden. When had things been this carefree?

"Honey, water the plants at the roots; that way, the sun won't scorch the leaves." She had no idea if that was true or not, but Aiden had told her to get the water to the roots, so it sounded reasonable.

Reasonable was another word she wasn't familiar with. It wasn't reasonable to stay with a man who abused her until she considered Kellyn. There was no way she'd leave her once she'd fallen in love with her. And falling in love with Kellyn had been instantaneous. From the beginning, her big brown eyes pleaded with Marina to stay. A silent scream for help.

She sipped her coffee and thought about Aiden. While it wasn't fair to compare the two men, she had to because Aiden was a part of their new lives, and Marina needed to make sure she protected herself. But mostly, she wanted to protect Kellyn.

Last night, when she'd spilled the fruit punch, she saw the type of man Aiden was. He didn't rage, lash out, or hit. He laughed and poured punch on himself on purpose to make sure Kellyn wasn't fearful. Rather than punish her and withhold her dinner, playtime, or another drink, he gave a fresh can and went about enjoying his dinner. That was what good looked like. It was important for Kellyn to see kindness in action.

Her eyes kept going next door, hoping to catch a glimpse of the man, but she knew he wasn't home. She'd peeked out the front door this morning and noticed his cruiser was gone. Like most people, he held a job and steady hours.

She wasn't used to that either. None of the Caswells fell into the normal realm. When your father was king, it granted a great deal of leeway to the family. Craig only went into the office when he was required to attend a meeting or show his face. No one complained because their lives were more pleasant when he wasn't around. His chief of police brother Chris had an abundance of deputies to cover for him while he perfected his golf game. Conrad, the youngest, was the only one who kept office hours, but that was because he answered to a higher power than his father, the mayor. He answered to the court system, and Mayor Caswell hadn't been able to fill those positions with his minions.

In the distance, her cell phone rang. It was an odd sound since few people had her number. Thinking it was one of Kellyn's doctors, she rose from the steps and raced into the kitchen to answer it. Caller ID showed an unlisted number.

Her skin crawled when Craig's voice sounded on the other end.

"Hello, Marina."

She swallowed the lump of fear that always choked her when she heard him speak.

"Craig." Her mind raced to figure out how he'd gotten her number. She had an agreement with his parents. If she didn't release the video of him beating her up with Kellyn cowering in the corner, they would leave her alone. "You calling isn't part of the agreement."

"Agreement? You and I never had an agreement."

She took a long fortifying breath. "Because

you're disagreeable. Listen, Craig, you can't call me."

"Oh, Mar Mar, haven't you learned anything yet? I do what I want."

She hated when he used his pet name for her. At first, she'd thought it sweet and cute that he gave her a nickname, but really he'd shortened it to reflect his power and control. He could do what he wanted, whether it was to rename her, ruin her, or, as his nickname reflected accurately, mar her.

She'd had over a month to heal since she left him. She'd spent that time getting her life sorted out. One of the things she'd changed was her number. "How you got my number, I don't understand, but you need to forget it. I want nothing to do with you."

She heard the crash of glass and knew he'd thrown something. "You don't get to choose. You took my daughter, and I want to see her."

All those months of martial arts classes straightened her spine. "Wrong. It's my life—my choice. You lost your options when you used your fists rather than your brain." She knew this conversation was going nowhere. Knew it was only a matter of time before he called or showed up. His father couldn't control him despite his promise to do so. One thing she also knew was she was ready for him.

"I hoped that the treatment facility would have helped."

"You bitch. You owe me forty-five days of my life."

She quickly calculated the time she'd spent married to him. "You owe me seven hundred and forty-six days of mine and all of Kellyn's. Don't call me again, or I swear I'll release the tape."

He laughed like he used to when he taunted her. "Do it, and it will be the last thing you do. Tell Kellyn her daddy loves her, and he'll see her soon." There was a click and then silence.

The only thing Marina heard was the whoosh of blood pounding through her veins, rushing to her ears. She let out a growl that vibrated the fear from her chest. There was no room for anxiety or panic. While she had the initial fight-or-flight response, she had to remind herself why she'd stayed so close to the crime scene.

Copper Creek was only forty minutes away, but that was where Kellyn's specialists were. They'd been making so much progress that Marina was certain changing everything for her daughter would set her back. Besides, Aspen Cove was where she wanted to be. It was the one place she could count on when she needed comfort or support.

When a hand pressed against her back, she reacted with all the pent-up frustration she'd stored inside. Whirling around, she yelled, "Leave me alone!" The words were meant for Craig, but they fell on tiny ears.

Kellyn stumbled back and landed on her bottom. Her face turned white, and her eyes filled with tears.

Marina ran to her daughter and pulled her into her arms. "Oh, Ladybug, I'm so sorry. You snuck up on me." She took a seat at the end of the couch and rocked her daughter until her tears ceased to fall. "I'm so sorry." Marina felt like a powder keg ready to explode. "We need a muffin or a cookie. What do you say?" She hated to run to the bakery every time, but it was the one place she could be surrounded by sweetness and love.

Kellyn wiped her runny nose on her sleeve and nodded. They grabbed their shoes and left. Kellyn needed a treat, and Marina needed a friend.

They arrived a few minutes later to find the bakery busy once again, but Katie spotted them and eyed the only empty table in the corner. Marina sat Kellyn down and went to get their sweets.

"What's wrong?" Katie's expression was filled with concern. She plated up a few cookies and a muffin and grabbed chocolate milk for Kellyn and a coffee for Marina.

"Nothing. It's all good."

Katie shook her head. "Does that work for others?"

"Does what work?"

The line had died down, and an older man came to the front to take over.

"Lying to yourself and getting everyone to believe it," Katie said.

She had to admit it was nice to have a friend who could see through her mask. "Yes, it generally works."

"Not with me. You look frazzled." She walked the plate of goodies to the table. "Kellyn looks like she could use a distraction too." Katie pulled her phone from her pocket and dialed a number. "You got room for one more?" There was a muffled reply. "Perfect. Kellyn's here. Just pick her up after you get Sahara."

"Wait. What?" Marina asked.

Katie laid her hand on top of Marina's. "I'm a mom. I know what overload looks like. You know Sage. She's got honorary aunt duty today. There's no reason she can't take Kellyn too."

"I couldn't impose." While an afternoon to herself sounded amazing, she didn't want to take advantage of anyone's kindness.

"This is Aspen Cove. There's no such thing as an imposition when you live among family."

Marina opened Kellyn's chocolate milk and put a straw into the container.

Family was a foreign concept to Marina. In her case, it was a single mother and a string of men who came and went. She didn't want that for Kellyn. It was probably why she'd fallen so hard and fast for her. It hadn't hurt that Craig had treated her like she was gold until he put a ring on her finger. At that time, Marina felt like she'd hit the jackpot. She had everything she'd dreamed about for a few minutes. When she said *I do*, it had all changed.

"I don't know what a family is supposed to look like. All I know is I'd do anything for her." She patted Kellyn's hair. Her daughter gave her a sweet smile. It was those smiles that made everything she'd gone through worth it.

"Family isn't always who you were born to. Sage is like a sister, and we aren't even related." Katie looked at Kellyn. "But you know that already. We're family. We take care of our own, and you look like you could use a break. Anything you want to talk about?"

Marina couldn't mention his name without sending her daughter into a fit of despair. "No, just got a call today." That was all she'd say because although Kellyn was only four, and she never spoke, she'd honed her other skills to perfection. She'd never met a more intuitive child in her life.

Katie frowned and nodded. "You know we'll circle the wagons."

"I know you'll try." It felt good to have a friend. The one thing abusers did was alienate their victims. It gave them power and control, so Marina wasn't used to having a support system.

The bell above the door rang, and Sage walked inside. It had been a long time since Marina seen the tiny redhead. She was the first person Marina had contact with after Bea, the original owner of the bed-and-breakfast, died. When Sage found her battered and bruised on the front steps over a year ago, she patched her up and gave her a room.

"You look amazing." Sage gave Marina a one-handed hug since her other arm helped balance the baby on her hip.

"Thanks, it's been a journey."

"I hear I'm getting a helper." Sage walked to where Kellyn sat at the table, drinking her chocolate milk and eating a cookie. "You want to come with me, little one? Sahara and I are going to watch cartoons and finger paint."

"The last time you finger painted with her, she ate more paint than she got on the paper," Katie said.

"Hey, you don't get to decide. Besides, I buy the nontoxic stuff, and Otis will lick them clean before you even get there."

"Right...the three-legged dog." Marina remembered the kind-hearted golden retriever. She leaned down and asked Kellyn if she wanted to visit the pup and paint. It didn't take long for her daughter to nod and gather her things. She was taking to her new life like a fish to water.

"Take your time. There's no rush to come and get her. We'll feed her and keep her entertained."

Marina smiled. It felt odd but comforting to know she could count on these women when she couldn't count on her own family. It wasn't that her mother was unreliable; she lived too far away. Sadly, she could never count on Craig's family to help.

"Ladybug, be good, okay?" She leaned into Sage and whispered, "She doesn't talk."

Sage smiled. "Sure she does; she just doesn't use words. We'll be fine."

She gave Sage her cell number and told her to call immediately if Kellyn pulled out a red cylinder from her bag.

Kellyn followed Sage outside.

For a few minutes, panic set in. In the past, when Marina didn't have Kellyn, it was usually because Craig dropped her off at a babysitter's so he could come home and beat her. She looked around, feeling vulnerable.

"She'll be okay." Katie rounded the counter and

wrapped Marina in a hug. "You're not alone anymore. Now, what are you going to do with yourself?"

It was a beautiful day. The sun sat high in the sky, but a cool mountain breeze kept it from becoming sweltering.

"I think I might find a tree in the park and just be me for a few minutes."

"That sounds amazing. Let me get you a snack." Katie boxed up a few muffins and put a bottle of water and a soda in a bag. "Just in case you need a little something." She walked her to the door and sent her on her way.

Marina drove the block to the park and found the perfect spot under a big oak tree. She lay on the grass and breathed the mountain air. She closed her eyes and let her senses take over. The heat of the sun poked through the leaves. The breeze swept the scent of pine and freshly mowed grass over her. Then she picked up something totally different in the air. She didn't have to open her eyes to know he was there. She had already memorized the smell of his citrus cologne.

CHAPTER EIGHT

Aiden stood over Marina and appreciated how peaceful she looked.

"You shouldn't sneak up on me." She opened her beautiful eyes and stared up at him. "I could be trained in martial arts."

"Are you?" He would love to see her kick ass, but then again, if she were trained in self-defense, she wouldn't have been mistreated.

"Maybe." She frowned at his uniform.

"I'll keep that in mind." He scouted the playground, looking for her daughter. "Where's Kellyn?"

"She's hanging out with Sage." Marina lifted to a seated position and leaned against the trunk of the tree. "Shouldn't you be working?"

He smiled and took a seat beside her. Far enough away he didn't crowd her but close enough to smell her coconut shampoo.

"I'm working. I saw a vagrant sleeping in the park and thought I'd check it out."

"And?"

"Turns out it's my cute neighbor enjoying some quiet time." A lone leaf floated down from the tree and landed on his trouser leg. He picked it up and stared at it thoughtfully. "Have you ever considered how nature naturally knows when to let go of the past and move forward?" He lifted the brown leaf. "Take this leaf for example. At one point, it took in water and nutrients from the sun and air, but now it's dried up. The tree knew it no longer needed it, so it set it free."

"Is there a lesson here?" She turned to face him and sat cross-legged. She picked up another leaf from the ground and ran her fingertips over the raised veins.

"No lesson. Just an observation." He tossed the leaf aside.

"I'm observant too. We're not talking about leaves and trees here, are we?"

He liked her. She was funny and kind and open, despite what he knew about her. This morning he'd taken another look at the information Mark had gathered. While there wasn't much, he knew she'd come out of a marriage that should have offered her untold wealth and opportunities, and yet she'd moved to Aspen Cove, a small town with little to offer. Her house was run-down, the siding peeled, the paint faded. The lawn hadn't been watered in years. The only thing that made it look occupied and alive were the plants he'd put in her garden.

"I'd love to hear your story."

"It's not all that exciting. Quite a common tale, I've been told."

He leaned against the trunk of the tree. "In all fairness, I need to tell you that my deputy ran a check on you."

Her eyes grew large and then narrowed to thin slits. "Is that standard practice?" She backed up several inches. "Do you spy on everyone who moves to town?"

Aiden hated that she put extra space between them. "No, and I didn't ask him to do it, but I'm glad he did. You want to tell me about the restraining order?"

She exhaled like a popped balloon. "Not really." Her shoulders tightened, her hands fisted. The mention of the restraining order obviously took her back to an awful place. Her body language was a perfect indicator.

"You're safe here."

She laughed. Not the ha-ha laugh that followed quick wit or easy banter, but the laugh that came with disbelief. "*Safe* is not a word in my vocabulary."

He scooted closer, watching her intently to see if she'd move away again. Relief surged through him when she didn't. "It is now. I can't imagine what you went through being married to a member of the Caswell family."

"You know them?"

He smiled. "We don't share meals. I wouldn't plant them a garden. I know of them, and I've had some run-ins with Chief Caswell and his brother Conrad. I'm not a fan."

She seemed to relax. "Me either."

"I won't press any further except to ask how bad was it, and should I be concerned?"

She yanked a few blades of grass from the ground. "It was terrible. I'd be lying if I told you it was over. As long as Craig is around, it will never be over."

Aiden filed that information away and risked another question. "What about the family? They couldn't help?"

Marina stretched her lips thin. "Oh, they could have, but they turned a blind eye. To help meant to acknowledge there was a problem. The Caswells have no problems. They are perfection personified."

"How did you get away?"

Her face lit up. "I learned how to play their game."

"Should I be worried about you?"

"No, I'm no threat to anyone unless they try to hurt me or my daughter."

He understood the need to protect. It was why he had become a police officer. A ladybug landed in her hair, and he reached forward to let it walk up his finger. He expected her to flinch, but she didn't. Not that she seemed comfortable with his movements. The way her body stiffened told him she was debating between fight and flight. He showed her the cute little bug.

"I love ladybugs. It's what I call Kellyn."

Aiden held his hand against Marina's, and the little polka-dotted bug moved from him to her. "Such happy-looking little things."

"That's my wish for her. I want her life to be free of worry. She's had it tough."

"Tell me about her?" While he would have liked to ask her pointed questions, he didn't want to risk the chance she'd stop talking to him.

He could tell she was unequivocally in love with her child. It seemed a no-brainer that a parent would be fully committed to their kid's happiness, but that wasn't always the case. He'd seen many parents not want the responsibility of nurturing and caring for their children.

"She's so smart. While I'm partial because she's mine, I'd put her at genius level."

He wondered how she judged the intelligence of a child who didn't speak. "Has she ever talked?" He leaned back until the bark bit lightly into his shirt.

"I've never heard her, but I'm told she has the sweetest voice and used to be a chatterbox with an advanced vocabulary."

That stumped Aiden. How could a mother not hear her child's voice? "I'm confused."

She nodded. "It's a long story, and it's complicated."

"I'd love to hear it." He glanced down at his uniform. "Why don't we have coffee tomorrow, and you can tell me not as the sheriff but as your friend."

Her hand raised to her chest. "Wow, I don't know what to say."

"Say yes to the coffee and to friendship."

Marina pinned her upper lip between her teeth for a moment and then nodded. "Coffee and friendship sound good."

"Perfect. How about the diner?"

She brushed off her jeans and stood. "How about the backyard? I don't want to talk in front of Kellyn. She needs to be protected. We can have coffee on the back porch while she plays in the garden."

Aiden thought about the yard and how little Kellyn had to entertain herself back there. An idea came to him. He'd have to sneak over again while they slept, but he liked his clandestine trips in the twilight hours. Seeing the looks on Marina's and Kellyn's faces was worth the lack of sleep.

"It's a date." When he saw the concern in her eyes, he continued, "Figure of speech. I'm not expecting anything but coffee."

She offered him her hand and tugged him to a standing position. She rocked back and forth on her heels. Seconds later, she lunged at him and gave him a quick hug.

"Thanks for being a good guy."

"My mom wouldn't have had it any other way."

She walked away, but before she got to her SUV, she turned and smiled. That was all it took to make his day.

AIDEN STOPPED at Bishop's Brewhouse. With so many people in town, the bar seemed to be the place people congregated. Poor Cannon had opened at noon to accommodate his patrons' needs. He'd hired a few townsfolk for the busier days like karaoke Friday or days he wanted to spend time with Sage.

"Hey, are things quiet?" He wasn't asking about the number of customers but the amount of trouble. With growth came the usual problems. There were more fights, more thefts, and more idiots. While crime didn't have an address, it seemed to move where opportunity was abundant.

Cannon stocked the back bar with bottles of liquor. "Yep, things are good. No drunks or fights, just idiots."

The few men at a corner table looked harmless. Dressed in camouflage, they were too early for hunting season, which didn't start until late August, so he figured they were here to fish. Aiden turned back to the bar where Cannon had put a cup of coffee in front of the second stool.

Sitting on the end stool was Mike. The one-eyed cat was more of a mascot than anything else—a good mouser, according to his owner. Aiden had heard that Cannon found the cat in a dumpster and brought it home. That seemed to be the way of the people who lived in Aspen Cove. They were rescuers, nurturers, and downright good folks. Aiden hoped that the growth wouldn't end his sweet, made-for-television life.

The door opened, and a group of construction

guys came in. They sat at a table in the center and ordered a pitcher of beer.

Cannon delivered and came back to stand in front of the sheriff. "What's new?"

He couldn't help the goofy smile that found its way to his face. "Got a new neighbor."

Cannon wiped down the counter. "Marina, right? Sage is practicing her parenting skills. She's got Sahara and Kellyn today."

Aiden leaned back. "Are you guys pregnant?"

Cannon let out a laugh that shook the wine-glasses hanging above him. "No, no, no, no. I can't even get that woman to the altar."

"Doesn't take a marriage license to make a baby." Aiden sipped his coffee and watched the group behind him in the mirror. They'd come in rowdy, and beer would not help.

"She likes to practice everything first."

"Practice is good. Practice makes perfect."

Cannon threw the damp towel into a nearby bucket; the water inside splashed over onto the counter. "We're so perfect, we could give lessons."

"What's the problem then?"

"You know her. She's got to plan it out a thousand times in her head."

"Don't wait for her. Set a date. Make sure she doesn't cook for the reception." While Sage was an excellent nurse, she couldn't cook a thing. Even microwaving was a challenge.

"Nope, I've already told Dalton he was on deck for the reception. It's great having a chef as one of your best friends. As for the date, I'm thinking Valentine's Day. It's super cliché, but deep inside, Sage loves all that romantic stuff."

"I'll put it on my calendar." Aiden took another drink of coffee. "What do you know about Marina?"

Cannon ran his hand through his hair before he shook his head. "Not much except she's shown up in town a few times looking like the loser in a prizefight. Be careful, man. She's got baggage. I'm not talking about a carry-on. That one has a steamer trunk full of problems."

"We've all got baggage."

The guys at the table lifted the empty pitcher and asked for another.

Cannon frowned. "You gonna be around for a bit?" He refilled Aiden's coffee mug and pulled another pitcher of beer.

"I've got your back for a while." His shift ended early today. Mark was coming in soon to take over.

He spun his seat around and gave the five men at the table a stern look. It was the one he used that said, *don't mess with me.*

"Sheriff," one idiot said. "Do you choose to wear shit-brown clothes, or is that the standard uniform?"

Aiden pushed himself from the stool and walked over to where they sat. "It's standard-issue. Brilliant choice, really. You see...when I kick the shit out of idiots, it hardly shows. What about you? You look good in orange?" He stared straight at the mouthiest of the bunch. He knew from experience if he silenced the loudest man, there wouldn't be a problem. It was herd mentality.

"Orange?"

Aiden pulled up a chair and straddled it, leaning his muscled arms on the back. "Yeah, it's the color we have at the local penitentiary." He moved his eyes from man to man. "I find that color doesn't go with many complexions. Shall I call ahead and reserve you a room and a uniform?"

Four of the men shook their heads and looked to their leader.

"We ain't done nothin' wrong."

Aiden stood. "Of course not. Are you planning to? I like to be prepared." He stood in front and looked down at the one guy he knew could turn his night into a nightmare.

"No, sir."

Aiden patted him on the back with more than friendly force. "Good to hear. You finish your beer, pay your tab, and we'll see you at the firehouse on Monday." It was his way of telling them he knew where they worked.

He returned to the bar. Mike had vacated the seat next to him. He looked around for the cat, but he'd disappeared. Probably because a one-eyed cat had the sense to leave when trouble was brewing.

"Thanks. Sage would be upset if she needed to patch me up as soon as I got home. Although, after she finished, she'd spend lots of time loving me."

Aiden emptied his coffee cup and put a few bucks on the counter. "You want me to give you a black eye?"

"Nah, I think I'll just stop by The Corner Store and pick up flowers. That's effective and less painful."

Aiden walked to the door and turned back to his friend. "You're a smart man."

"I'm still in training."

Aiden chuckled. "Smarter because you know that and don't fight it."

He walked into the afternoon sun. After a quick check-in at the office, he drove to Copper Creek to get a long length of rope and a piece of wood.

CHAPTER NINE

Her stomach fluttered as if a kaleidoscope of butterflies raced through her insides. When was the last time she'd experienced anything remotely like this? What was this? Nerves...excitement... She didn't know how to gauge her reactions and responses. All she'd known the past two years was fear and relief. This was not that.

Marina stood in front of her closet and thumbed through her clothes. She'd donated most of her things to the shelter because every outfit came with a memory and rarely a pleasant one. She'd never forget the day she took Kellyn to the thrift store. Her eyes lit up like she'd been invited to a party. A place where everything from toys to tennis shoes was available and affordable. It was where she got her collection of books, Legos, and puzzles.

The only things they took from the house were her safety blocks and Mrs. Beasley. A person couldn't move into the future if they were living in the past.

A tug on her nightshirt brought her eyes down to her little girl, who held out two dresses, one yellow and one red.

"You choose. You look pretty in both."

Kellyn looked between the two and pointed to the ladybug on the yellow dress.

"That's the perfect choice. Don't forget Mr. Cooper is coming over for coffee this morning."

Kellyn gave her a thoughtful look and then nodded before she skipped back to her room. It was amazing the changes that were happening with her in such a short period. Weeks ago, she stayed in the shadows. She never spoke. She rarely engaged either. Marina was the only person she'd relax around. The only person who could touch her, and yet she spent an entire afternoon with Sage and Sahara.

While Marina knew being around baby Sahara had influenced her decision, she was proud that her daughter was showing signs of life. Signs that she was indeed a four-year-old child despite her wise and wary eyes.

She pulled a pale-blue sundress from the hanger and slipped it over her head. She checked herself in the mirror twice before she rolled her eyes. *It's coffee, not a date.* The thought of a date terrified her. She couldn't trust her instincts when it came to men. However, Aiden Cooper wasn't like most men. What made him different she couldn't figure out, but he was.

Maybe it was because his smile always reached his eyes. Could be that he took his job to serve and protect seriously. Probably was because he understood that when a four-year-old little girl planted a dead daisy into the ground, she expected it to grow, and he made that happen. They hardly knew him, and he'd shown more kindness than her ex ever had.

Marina slicked on some gloss and walked to the kitchen. She'd wanted to do something special in the garden, like set up a table, but she didn't have the resources, so he'd have to settle for coffee on the steps. Just as she was getting ready to pull the curtains open to peek into the garden, a knock sounded at the front door.

Was he always early?

Kellyn stood in the hallway, peeping around the doorframe. She wouldn't come out unless she knew it was safe.

Even Marina took extra precautions like checking the peephole to confirm identity. While her ex-in-laws had promised Craig wouldn't be a problem, Marina knew there was no way they'd be able to watch him all the time. Hell, they'd known what was going on and did nothing until she threatened to go public, which would have ruined the mayor's run for reelection. That was her godsend. She shook the thoughts from her mind and opened the door to Aiden, who was so darn handsome in simple jeans and a T-shirt.

"Hey, you're early."

He shrugged. "Old habits die hard. My mom used to tell me that early was on time and on time was late." He lifted a B's Bakery bag. "I brought breakfast if you haven't eaten. A snack if you have."

Where did this man come from? "Come on in. I was making the coffee when you knocked." She stepped to the side and allowed him to enter—a huge step for her. By the smile on Aiden's face, she knew he understood what a big deal it was for him to be in their home.

"Where's the little bug?" He looked around and saw her tiny face peeking around the corner. "Good morning, Kellyn. I have a surprise for you."

Marina led him into the kitchen. "What have you been up to now?"

He chuckled. It was a warm sound that seemed to come straight from his heart.

She glanced behind him to see Kellyn slipping along the walls to get closer.

"I'm ashamed to say more trespassing, but I do know the sheriff, and he can vouch for my character and motives."

Marina had no idea what else the man could have done. He'd planted a full garden for her and a daisy garden for Kellyn. She started the pot of coffee and pulled the curtains above the sink open. Her heart danced when she saw what he'd done.

Tears sprang to her eyes as her chest tightened and twisted. Not the kind of pain that came from fear or anxiety, but the kind that came from an over-flowing heart. Hanging from the big oak tree out back was a swing for Kellyn.

She tried to speak, but the words caught in her throat, so she did something unusual. She threw her arms around Aiden and hugged him tightly. He tentatively wrapped his around her and pulled her into a friendly embrace.

She felt safe. Safe enough to stay there for a minute too long to enjoy the feel of his hands on her back. Take in the smell of his cologne. Soak in the heat of his body. It wasn't until she felt a tug at the hem of her dress that she realized how long she'd let the hug last.

She glanced down at Kellyn and smiled.

"I'm so sorry, but I'm so moved." She swooped

Kellyn into her arms and pointed to the tree. The little girl's eyes grew as big as baseballs as she wiggled out of Marina's arms and raced to the door. Her hand had barely reached the brass knob when she turned around and bolted to Aiden, throwing her arms around one of his legs. Her impromptu squeeze lasted a second before she took off again for the door and the swing.

"She may be in love with you."

Aiden laughed. "I don't date women that young," he teased.

Marina poured two cups of coffee. "Good to know." She walked out back and took a seat on the top step. "I'd offer you a seat, but I don't have any."

"Hang tight." Aiden skipped down the steps and cleared the fence separating the two yards with a simple hop. In less than a minute, he was back with three folding chairs. "Not fancy, but they work."

Marina took a sip of her coffee and sat in the chair he offered. He took the one beside her, leaving the other vacant for Kellyn. "I've had fancy, and it's not all it's cracked up to be. Thanks for the chairs and the muffins." She looked at Kellyn, who pumped her legs, trying to get the swing to move. "Most of all—" she swallowed the lump in her throat and pointed to the swing "—thanks for that. She's really coming out of her shell around you."

"I'm glad. I'd like to spend more time with both of you." He looked at her with earnest eyes.

Her first instinct was to tell him it would never work out, but she wasn't sure if that was true. He'd done nothing but be nice to them. He wasn't asking to marry her; he was asking for her friendship. Friendship was free—something she could afford.

After a long pause, she answered, "I'd like that." Then looked back at her daughter. "We'd like that."

He stood and took a step toward Kellyn. "You want a push?" He didn't move another step in her direction until her little head bobbed in a nod.

In long strides, he reached her to give her a gentle nudge. Just enough momentum to get her started, and she did the rest.

Aiden returned to his chair. He leaned forward, then leaned back. Something about his posture told her he needed more information. It wasn't every day a skittish woman with a silent child moved into the house next door. Give her the last name Caswell and a restraining order, and there was definitely a story to tell.

"You can ask," she said.

Immediately, his tense shoulders softened. "The Caswells?"

Talk of them always made her throat tight and her mouth dry. "They aren't good people."

She could see the wheels rotating in his head.

The question could have been written on his forehead.

"How bad was Craig?"

"Worst of the bunch." She reached into the bag and pulled out a muffin. Saturday meant apple spice. "Although I wasn't married to any of the others, so I can't say for sure."

"Why'd you stay?"

She looked at her baby on the swing. "Her. I stayed for her."

He nodded. "I understand."

Marina shook her head. "I don't think you do. I don't think you understand the significance of what having her with me means."

He twisted his body, so he faced her and leaned back. "You don't have to tell me anything you don't want me to know."

One more look at the joy on Kellyn's face as she swung told Marina she owed him at least her story.

"I want to tell you, but first you need to understand that while I may be a victim of domestic abuse, I feel like a victor. I refuse to let what happened to me define who I am and who she is."

He sat taller. "I respect that."

"I married Craig Caswell two years ago after dating only a few weeks." She could see by the tilt of his head that he knew the math wasn't right. "Clearly, you're a mathematician."

"It doesn't add up."

"It will."

He looked toward the big oak tree. "Okay, so how did you get out of the marriage with her?"

"I blackmailed them."

CHAPTER TEN

Few things surprised Aiden. He'd been a cop in a big city where shocking things happened every day, but never did he expect that answer. Most people didn't confess to blackmail. It was a crime, and he was a cop. "Why would you tell me that?"

"Why?" She split her muffin and offered him half. "I guess you could say I feel safe with you. Safe enough to divulge my secrets."

He took a bite and stayed silent while he swallowed the muffin and chewed on her confession. "Do you have lots of secrets?"

"No, and I don't make it a habit to blackmail people. It was a necessary evil. I got the idea while eating a muffin in B's Bakery. I got the resources for my plan by turning Indigo, the pop star, back into

Samantha White, the woman. I dyed her blue hair back to brown, and she paid me way too much money. Money I'll forever be grateful to have had."

He shook his head. "I'm confused."

"I can see why. Shall I give you the short version?"

While the short version might satisfy his need for quick answers, something told him the long version would be best. "Start from the beginning."

She let out a sigh. "One would think I married for the money. I didn't. I was a hairdresser, and he came into my shop one day." She looked to the blue sky as if the answers were there. "We talked while I cut his hair. He was charming, as all sociopaths are. He told me he was a divorcé and had a little girl. Her mother had abandoned her. He showed me Kellyn's picture. God, Aiden, she was so tiny and looked so sad."

"So, you fell for a picture?"

She smiled. "Yeah, I guess I did. How could a mother abandon her little girl? On my wedding night, I knew why. He beat the living hell out of me. It was his way of showing me who was boss."

"And you stayed?"

"How could I leave? Here was this little girl, so traumatized by her yet-to-be-lived life. I knew I could make a difference. If I didn't, who would?"

"Did you file a report? Seek any kind of help?"

She stared at him like he'd grown horns. "I'm not stupid. The next morning, I drove down to the police station. I had a black eye and swollen lip and a hundred other bruises that couldn't be seen. The biggest to my heart and ego."

"Let me guess. You were taken to Chris?" He used the chief's first name because it was easier to keep things straight.

"You know the story." She lowered her voice to a baritone. "We don't air our dirty laundry in the community. Internal problems are solved internally. Go home, Marina, and make your husband happy." Her voice took on its normal sweet tone. "I went home and tried to make it work until I couldn't."

He fisted his hands. He wanted to hit something. Someone—Chief Chris Caswell, but when she saw him tense up, so did she, so he forced the tension to leave his body. She needed reassurance that he was different. "I'm so sorry. You didn't deserve that."

"No, I didn't, but neither did she. I don't know if he ever hit her. All I know is he didn't when I was there. I can't blame her mother for leaving; it was awful, but she should have taken Kellyn with her."

"How'd you get her away from them?"

"I showed them indisputable evidence of which there were many copies."

"You got video?" God, she was brilliant. Most

people in those situations couldn't think past the last attack. Often they were trying to figure out what they could do to avoid the next one. Marina had known it was coming and used it to free herself.

"I did. You've got to love a nanny cam. The only reason I got away with it was because it's an election year and Mayor Caswell expects to win."

"What a family."

"Oh yeah, real pillars of the community. After I turned over one copy to each of the Caswells, Craig went on a long vacation to a rehab center. I got a quickly processed annulment courtesy of the district attorney. I also received full custody of Kellyn. The only stipulation was that I stay in the state. It wasn't because they wanted access to her. In truth, the Caswells don't do damaged. They do the damage. In their eyes, Kellyn is broken, and broken things are discarded. They want me close to control me."

"I imagine they have a gag order in place." His mind took notes as fast as she gave information.

"No, more of a gentleman's agreement to stay silent. They didn't want a paper trail. The only thing I have in writing is the restraining order because I demanded it. It's hard to find unless you have access to those types of things. It's buried deep in the system." She gave him a like-you-did look.

"It wasn't me, but it was my overzealous deputy. I'm sorry he crossed the line."

"I'm not. Someone should know the whole story. You're the only one who does."

He reached out and covered her hand with his. "Thank you for trusting me. I know how hard that must be."

She looked to where his hand lay on top of hers and turned hers over. It was no longer a single-sided gesture. She weaved her fingers through his until they held each other's hands. "I have to start somewhere. I started with you."

They watched Kellyn swing, and Aiden liked how this moment felt. There was no need for words; the silence was perfect.

Minutes later, Kellyn jumped off and went to check on her daisies.

"You've given her more than her father ever did."

Aiden scooted his chair closer to Marina. "I'll give her more if she'll let me." He turned toward Marina. "I'd love to take you both on a date. A real date. How about we go to Sam's Scoops for ice cream later? And if you're up to it, I'd love to make dinner for you both."

He expected to see fear or uncertainty in Marina's soulful blue eyes, but he found neither. If he wasn't too far off the mark, he swore he saw hope and the sparkle of excitement.

"I'm a definite yes, but we'll have to get the boss on board." Without taking her hand from his, she pulled him down the stairs toward Kellyn. "Hey, Ladybug?"

She stood and handed a white daisy to Marina. Her eyes went to Aiden, and she plucked another flower and gave it to him.

He knew she wouldn't be a hard sell either. The only thing Kellyn needed was to know she was safe. It dawned on him that she'd left the house without her colored blocks. Was that because she felt safe in her yard or safe in general? It would be interesting to see.

He kneeled down so he was at her height. "Thank you for the flower, Kellyn. I love when you give them to me. I still have the other one in a vase on my table." Marina gave him an is-that-true look.

"Cross my heart. I've got it in a glass jar on my table because it's so special." He risked reaching out and touching her. His hand moved toward the hair that had fallen in her face.

She stood still as if she were challenging herself not to cower.

He brushed the long strands of her hair from her pretty brown eyes. "I hoped I could take your mom and you for an ice cream this afternoon. What do you think? Would you like ice cream?"

Her expression turned from one of apprehension to joy. She looked up at Marina, who laughed.

"I already told him yes for me. I'm not missing out on ice cream but choose for yourself. If you say no, I'll stay with you. It's perfect either way. We can get ice cream at The Corner Store together. No matter what, I win because I get you."

Aiden loved that Marina didn't press her to choose a certain way. Many parents manipulated their kids in the direction they wanted to go. Marina told her the truth. She'd love to get ice cream with him, but the world would not end if they didn't.

Kellyn seemed excited but undecided. He would have loved for her to open her mouth and scream that she wanted ice cream, but the fact she considered it gave him hope.

Aiden stood. "Tell you what. I've got stuff to take care of." He looked to his yard. "The weeds never stop growing. You girls decide if you want ice cream, and if you do, I'll meet you out front in two hours."

Kellyn looked to where his and Marina's hands were still together. When she glanced up, he swore he saw her smile for the briefest of moments. He reluctantly let her hand go and walked to the fence, where he hopped over.

He went to work on his garden after days of neglect. An hour later, he'd removed the weeds that choked the life out of his squash and cucumbers. He'd peeked over several times to find Kellyn at the chain-link fence watching him.

If she were older, he would have told her how life was like a garden. You reaped what you sowed. Nothing happened if you didn't plant the seeds of friendship and fertilize with happiness and love. Nothing grew if you didn't water and nurture it. And sometimes, outside forces moved in to damage what you started. He would have told her that Craig Caswell and his family were weeds that had been plucked from her life for good.

With thirty minutes left, he put away his tools and went inside his house to shower. If he was fortunate enough to have a date with the two prettiest girls in Aspen Cove, he wanted to look good and smell better.

CHAPTER ELEVEN

Kellyn took the date thing seriously. She'd changed her dress twice and actually brushed her hair, which rarely happened without a fight. She hated it when Marina had to tug at the knots, but today she sat patiently while Marina braided it and put a bow on top.

"You look pretty, sweetie."

Marina had also changed her clothes. She wished she'd had time for a shower, but after they spent the first hour playing in the yard, she took the next to go over her dismal finances. While she had enough money to cover next month's rent, the following month wouldn't be so easy if she didn't get a few clients. She would have to get the word out she was open for business, even if it was only haircuts in her kitchen.

Five minutes before they were due outside, Kellyn picked up Mrs. Beasley and walked to the door.

"I'm coming." Marina grabbed her purse, and they were leaning against Aiden's red Mustang when he walked out looking like a model. She'd seen a lot of public servant calendars. Hell, she used to get the Aussie fire department calendar each year and hang it at her station in the salon. She told people it was because she loved the puppies. Their eyes would get big as they thumbed through the pages saying, "There were puppies?"

"Look at you two." Aiden locked his front door and hopped off his porch. "You have her booster seat?"

She pointed to back of the car where she'd left it on the driveway. She loved that he paid attention. Could be because he was a cop, but she knew it was more than that. Aiden seemed to pay attention to the important stuff. She'd promised herself that she'd never rely on a man again, but maybe she'd been hasty with that statement. Maybe she should amend it to be she would never rely on a man not worthy of her. Aiden was the type of man she could trust. She felt it deep in her bones.

He strapped the booster into the back seat and

stood aside as Marina buckled Kellyn in. Sam's Scoops was a good thirty minutes away. They were barely five minutes outside of town when she turned around to find her baby sound asleep with Mrs. Beasley tucked in her arms.

"She's out like a light."

"All that swinging can wear a kid out."

Marina turned toward him. "When did you do it?"

He glanced quickly in her direction before putting his eyes back on the road. "When did I do what?"

"The swing. When did you put it in the tree, and how is that I never know you're sneaking around my yard?"

"Early this morning. You don't hear me because your room's at the front of the house."

They drove with the top down. The wind blew through her hair. Nothing had ever felt so good.

"She loves it. So do I."

"I'm glad. Isn't it time you had some nice things happen to you?"

"I could use nice." She considered all the things she needed. Nice was certainly one of them. Another was work. "I could use some clients. If you know anybody who needs a haircut, a perm, or a color, send them my way."

Aiden laughed. "I gave up perms long ago, but I could use a trim."

"Done. On the house."

"Not on your life. I'm a paying customer."

She frowned at him. "Sorry, but no, you can't plant my garden, bring us muffins, install a swing, and not let me do something for you in return."

He reached over and held her hand. "Marina, you're in this car with me, and that's the best reward. You're sharing your daughter and your time." He squeezed her hand gently. "I didn't do those things because I expected something in return."

Her heart skipped a beat. The last time it did that was when she came out of Kellyn's therapy session and found Craig standing on the corner, but this was different. Her heart leaped with joy knowing that she could enjoy time with a man and not fear for her life or safety. She hadn't been sure it would ever be possible. It might not have been if the man wasn't Aiden Cooper.

"I'm not offering to cut your hair because I feel like I owe you. I want to give you a haircut because it's the one way I can give something back—a way to water the friendship garden." She lifted a brow. "Maybe I just want to run my fingers through your hair."

"Is that right?" He pulled her hand to his lips

and kissed the back. "You can do that anytime you want."

She was certain her face was beet red because a wave of heat raced from her cheeks to her core. It was another thing she never thought she'd feel again —desire. It had been months since her annulment. Almost half a year since she'd had sex. Over two years since she'd had it willingly. Never in her wildest imagination did she think she'd feel the passion course through her veins like it did when Aiden was near.

Was it because he was kind and generous? Maybe because he was sexy. All she knew was she liked the way it felt. For the first time in a long time, she experienced normal.

They pulled into a dirt turnout off the highway. To the side sat a half dozen picnic tables, and smack dab in the center was a trailer with a sign that hung from the open window that read Sam's Scoops.

Kellyn woke when the engine stopped. She sat up and took in her surroundings.

"Are you ready for some ice cream, Princess?" Aiden reached in and unbuckled her. She went immediately into his arms. It was obvious it shocked him by the look of surprise on his face, but he settled her on his hip as if he'd done it a million times. With his free hand, he twined his fingers with Marina's and led them to the window.

"Fair warning," he said. "The names are crazy, but the ice cream is good. Although it might say ants or poop or something insane in the description, there really isn't anything gross in the mix."

There were three flavors available.

Honeycomb Your Hair, which was bits of honeycombs in vanilla ice cream, served in a bowl of cotton candy.

Beds Bugs, which was chocolate ice cream with chocolate-covered peanuts, drizzled with caramel syrup.

Princess and the Pooper, which was rainbow sherbet sprinkled with Pop Rocks and a dollop of fudge.

"How fun," Marina said. She turned to Kellyn, who was still in Aiden's arms. Mrs. Beasley hung from her hand, the tiny yellow feet of the doll almost hitting the ground. "Do you want hair, bugs, or poop?"

Her tiny face scrunched up as if they all sounded awful. Listing the names the way she had made them sound appalling.

"I'll have the Honeycomb Your Hair," Marina said.

"I'm all over the Bed Bugs," Aiden added.

As a four-year-old, it was probably hard for Kellyn to separate real from fake.

"Tell you what, let's get all three flavors and

share. Kellyn can have the first bite and decide which she likes the best. If there's one she falls in love with, it's all hers. If not, we can share. I don't mind sharing my Bed Bugs."

Marina appreciated his diplomacy. "Sounds great."

"What's it going to be?" the old man in the window asked. His eyes grew wide in recognition when Aiden stepped up. "Sheriff Cooper, I didn't know you had a family."

Aiden looked at Marina and Kellyn, and he didn't correct the man; he simply smiled. "Hey, Sam, my girls want ice cream, and so we'll have one of each."

"Extra ants?" Sam asked.

When no one answered, Aiden said, "Sure, we love ants."

Marina carried two of the bowls while Aiden carried Kellyn and the third bowl to the picnic table. He got Kellyn and Mrs. Beasley settled before he rounded the table and sat by Marina.

He handed out spoons. "Okay, on the count of three, dig into the one that looks best. One...two...three."

The spoons flew through the air to the center of the table with both Marina and Aiden digging into the Bed Bugs while Kellyn went for the Princess and the Pooper.

Marina swallowed a bite and groaned. "Oh my God, I never thought I'd say I want more bed bugs."

Kellyn scooped up a bite of the chocolate and hummed. It was the first time she'd made a sound in months. Marina thought she'd heard her whisper to her doll occasionally, but she never spoke or made a peep in front of a person. The unexpected sound filled her heart with happiness.

Once they finished their ice cream, Aiden took them back to Aspen Cove and to Hope Park. They played with Kellyn until their stomachs grumbled for something more substantial. They left Aiden's car by the park and walked hand in hand to Maisey's Diner.

For a Saturday, the place was busy, but Maisey had an open booth in the corner.

"Hey, y'all, I'd recommend the blue-plate special if you want to eat this year," she said. "It's chicken-fried steak, mashed taters, and gravy." She looked at Kellyn. "You look like a grilled cheese and tater tot kind of gal to me. Sound good?"

"Perfect for Kellyn and me." Marina turned toward Aiden. "What about you?"

"I love Maisey's chicken-fried steak. Sold!"

The best thing about the blue-plate specials was there was never a wait. Their meals arrived quickly.

Marina put her napkin in her lap. "You know so much about us, Aiden. What about you?"

He swallowed the bite he was chewing. "Not much to tell. I'm an only child. My father was a good man. Also, a police officer."

"Was?"

"Yes, he was a thirty-year veteran of the Colorado Springs Police Department. Made it to retirement and died a week after when a drunk driver hit him head-on."

"Oh God, Aiden. I'm so sorry."

Aiden sipped his soda. "I'm a lucky man." He looked at Kellyn. "My father was wonderful and an excellent role model, and I had him for the most important years of my life. He lives inside me each day, whispering words of wisdom."

"How'd you get here from Colorado Springs?"

"Lucky, I guess. I got shot. Should have been a simple speeding ticket, but it wasn't. There was a stolen car and a chase." He rubbed his right shoulder. "I had a girlfriend, and she found comfort with another—my partner."

"Oh, no." She leaned into him and wrapped her hands around his arm. His was solid, muscular, and his strength felt good under her fingertips.

"It was a good lesson. Probably not as physically painful as yours, but it hurt. I didn't want a constant reminder each time I walked into the precinct, so I healed and found another opportunity. I've been here and happy ever since. Aspen Cove is exactly where I want to be."

They finished their meal while talking about the town, its residents, and the recent growth. Aiden took his wallet out and paid. She wanted to offer to help, but she knew he'd never allow it, and her resources were limited.

On their way back to the car, she stopped at the vacant beauty shop to look in the whitewashed windows.

"You should see if you can open this place again. The town can use someone with your skills."

Marina laughed. "I can barely pay my rent. There's no way I'd be able to lease an entire shop."

"You'd be surprised at how generous this town can be." Rather than walk to the park, he led them to the bakery where Katie was getting ready to close the doors. "Wait up. We've got a wall wish."

Katie held the door open while the three of them filled out sticky notes and stuck them to the board that read The Wishing Wall. Marina opened Kellyn's because she was curious to see what her daughter had put on her paper. In the center was a heart. One single heart that told Marina Kellyn's was healing. She didn't dare look at Aiden's. His wish was his own, but hers said she needed clients.

They arrived at her house, and Aiden removed the booster and put it back in Marina's SUV. They stood on the front of her porch like shy teens. After a minute, he stepped back.

"I had a great time today. One of the best since I came to town," he said. He kneeled down in front of Kellyn. "Thanks for the date. We'll plan another one soon." He rose and leaned forward and gave Marina a kiss on the cheek. The heat of his lips touched her skin. It was a delicious burn that traveled to her heart.

"Best date of my life, Aiden." She looked down at her daughter. "I should get her bathed and in bed. She's had a full day."

He turned and walked to his house.

She watched him until he disappeared inside.

"Let's go, Ladybug. It's a bath and a bedtime story for you." She went through their nightly routine with a smile on her face. Poor Kellyn only made it halfway through *Goodnight Moon* when her heavy lids closed.

Marina was in the kitchen when her phone rang. As soon as she saw the mayor's number, she considered not answering, but ignoring his call would be like poking a bear.

"Hello," she answered.

"Hello, Marina. It's me again."

The anger at hearing Craig's voice scorched her insides. They roiled and rumbled until the acid rose to burn her throat. "Craig, you're not—"

"Shh, don't say it," he warned. "I've missed you, and I'd like to see my daughter."

She knew she couldn't trust the Caswells. They'd broken their first agreement. He'd called from his father's line. It was his way of proving no one could control him.

"You can't call me."

"But I did, and there's nothing you can do."

He was right because nothing in the restraining order prohibited Mayor Caswell from calling. It was her word against theirs. "Tell your father thank you," she said with sarcasm.

"I will when we have breakfast tomorrow. We'll miss you, but I want you to bring Kellyn."

She hated the Sunday breakfasts she'd been forced to endure while she was married. "That's not part of the agreement."

"I want a new agreement. If you recall, I didn't actually have a say in the last one. Decisions were made for me."

"There won't be a new agreement. Leave me alone."

There was a moment of silence before he said, "I'll never leave you alone. By the way, how is Aspen Cove treating you? Cute little place you got. Looks like tenement housing."

Her heart tumbled into the pit of her stomach, and she couldn't listen to another word. Hanging up the phone, she raced to the back porch to get fresh air and space. She was close to a panic attack and possibly a complete mental breakdown. A good cry was seconds away, and she refused to wake Kellyn and fill her world with worry.

She sat on the top step, buried her head in her hands, and wept. How could a day go from heaven to hell so fast?

CHAPTER TWELVE

Aiden stepped onto his back porch with a beer in his hand and a smile on his face. He couldn't re-member a time when he'd had so much fun. Every minute he spent with Marina and Kellyn was better than the last.

She appreciated everything he did, while his ex had appreciated nothing until it was gone.

He leaned over the deck rail and breathed in the night-blooming jasmine, its scent a perfect end to a sweet day.

He heard her before he saw her. A muffled cry came from Marina's back steps. His initial response was to jump the fence and go to her rescue, but what if he'd caused her unhappiness? He ran the entire day through his head. There was nothing that should have caused her to cry.

He set his beer on the two-by-four wood rail and made his way to the fence.

"You okay?" he called out.

Her head lifted from the curled-up ball she'd rolled herself into. She swiped at her cheeks and sat up.

"Yes, I'm great."

Aiden knew what great looked like. It was when her eyes danced with joy. When she smiled at eating ice cream called Bed Bugs and when Kellyn let him pick her up. That was great. Her sitting on the back stairs alone with a stream of tears running down her cheeks was nowhere close.

He hopped the fence and walked to where she sat on the step, taking up the space beside her. While he wanted to pull her into his arms, he didn't want to overstep his boundaries.

"You want to talk about it?"

She swallowed hard. "Not really."

"Is Kellyn okay?" He placed his hand on her back and moved his palm in a slow circle.

"She's asleep. She had the best day. I swear I even heard her giggle a time or two." She shook while she tried to control the next bout of tears.

"Hey." *Damn the distance.* "Come here and let me hold you." He opened his arms and prayed she would fall into them. When she did, he wrapped her in a hug. "Let me help you."

She cried for a few minutes. A few jagged breaths later, she began. "He won't leave me alone."

Anger as hot as lava boiled inside him. He didn't need a name to know who she was talking about. "What happened?"

"He called." She scooted closer.

She was inches from sitting in his lap. God, he wanted to pull her there.

"That breaks his restraining order. I can have him arrested."

She sat up and pushed away. Fear was written all over her face. "No. He's smarter than that. He used his father's phone. He wants to see Kellyn."

That was the last thing Kellyn needed. He'd watched her bloom and grow over the short time she'd been here. Seeing her father would no doubt cause the little newfound spark of happiness to wither and die.

"What did you tell him?"

She laid her head against his chest and took in a big breath. "I told him no."

"That's my girl." He hugged her tightly. She needed to know she wasn't alone in this. "Hold your ground."

"He knows I'm in Aspen Cove. He knows

where I live." Her voice cracked, ready to break into a sob once more.

"That's okay. I won't let him hurt you or Kellyn again." He took a chance and lifted her into his lap so he could hold her. "I've got you." He buried his nose in her hair and breathed in her tropical shampoo. "It's going to be okay."

She nodded against his chest and stayed in his arms. The ragged breaths turned even and slowed.

"Where did you come from, Aiden?"

"Colorado Springs."

She pulled back to look at him. Her fingers traced the design on his T-shirt. "No, I mean, how did you turn out to be such a nice guy?"

He chuckled. "Am I?" His hands rubbed her arms to keep her warm.

"The nicest. Where were you two years ago?"

"I was right here waiting for you. You're late." He lifted a hand to her chin. "Where were you?"

"I was living in hell."

Aiden smiled and leaned in. He couldn't help himself as he brushed his lips tentatively across hers. "Welcome to heaven, baby." He thumbed the remaining tears from her cheeks. It killed him that Craig had taken the smile he'd left earlier and turned it into a frown. "Can I kiss you?"

She looked at him like he was speaking in tongues. "You just did."

"Oh, Marina. That wasn't a kiss."

She squirmed in his lap, which made the desire he felt for her hard to hide. Then again, he wanted their relationship to start with honesty, and his body responded truthfully.

"Why do you like me? I'm a mess."

"You're a beautiful mess with an amazing daughter. I like everything about you." He readjusted her on his lap, hoping to make them both more comfortable. "And look what you do to me."

She shifted her hips until his length pressed against the back of her thigh. "Oh my. I'm not—"

"I'm not asking for anything but a kiss, and if you say no, I'll wait until I can convince you I'm kiss-worthy."

She looked at the garden and then to the swing. "You're already kiss-worthy."

He stared at her lips. "I didn't do those things because I expected something in return. I did them for me because it makes me feel good to make you smile. I want you to kiss me because you want to, not because you feel obligated to pay for my kindness. My kindness is free, Marina. No strings attached."

She brushed her finger across his lower lip.

He wanted to open his mouth and suck it inside, but he stayed still. Holding Marina was like holding a bird with an injured wing. There was no doubt she'd heal and be able to fly again. It was a matter of how much nurturing she'd need before she tried.

"What about your kisses? Are they free too?" she asked.

"Only for you."

"You charge everyone else?"

He tugged her closer, leaving his hands on her hips. She was perfect in his arms. He knew her kisses would be magical on his lips. "Now that would be illegal, and I walk the line on the side of the law. Nope, these lips have decided they want your kisses. What do you say?"

She cupped his face with her palm. In her eyes were a thousand emotions, but the one most recognizable was desire. "I say, kiss me."

He'd hoped that would be her answer, but he hadn't expected it. He wanted their first kiss to be special. He framed her face with his hands. "You're beautiful." He thumbed the small scar on her cheek. "There's something about you that speaks to my heart and soul."

She leaned forward. Her lips were a breath away from his. "I don't know how to do this anymore."

He dropped his hand to her breastbone. "Trust your heart. Trust me. Ask me for anything, and I'll always give you more."

"Kiss me," she whispered.

He slid his hand behind her neck to support the back of her head.

Boom.

Boom.

Boom.

His heart beat like a drum. When his fingers threaded softly through her hair, his lips touched hers. The kiss was soft until she pulled him closer to deepen it.

Her mouth opened with a moan as his tongue dipped inside to taste her honeyed sweetness. Nothing had ever been this right.

Aiden had kissed plenty of women in his lifetime, but none had made his heart twist and tighten in the process. None had made his stomach flip and flop. None had made him want to climb mountains or slay dragons. That's exactly what Marina's kiss did to him. It made him want to do whatever it took to protect her.

His fingers itched to feel her body, but for tonight, a kiss would have to be enough. They separated to catch a breath and pressed their lips together again. Marina was a passionate woman denied for far too long.

He moaned when they parted again.

She reached up to touch her lips like somehow the kiss had changed them. "You should charge for those kisses. You could make a fortune."

His heart picked up a beat. "You like my kisses?"

She nodded. "Might be the best kiss of my life."

"Might be?" He wanted to leave her with a solid opinion, not a maybe. "Better give it another whirl. I want you to be certain."

This time the kiss was deeper, longer, and more passionate. His tongue floated across hers like he was savoring every second, which he was. Kissing Marina would by far be his favorite pastime. When the kiss ended, and they looked at each other, he saw that he'd replaced her sadness with hope.

She sat back and stared at him. "Verdict is in. That was by far the best kiss I've ever had."

He gave her a quick peck on the lips. "I'm not even warmed up yet."

She shivered. "Neither am I." The goose bumps covering her arms showed how cold she was.

As much as he didn't want her to leave, he knew she needed to get warm. "You should go inside."

The look on her face said she'd rather stay out here and freeze.

"It's hard to go inside when I know those kisses are waiting out here. I'd love to invite you in, but with an impressionable four-year-old, it's not the right thing to do."

"As much as I'd love to sit on that couch and kiss you silly, you're right. There's more than us and kisses to think about." He knew the second her thoughts went back to the call. The light left her eyes, and her smile fell into a tight, stretched line. "Hey." He moved her off his lap and stood, pulling her up with him. "You don't have to worry about him. I'm here. I'm not going anywhere."

She gave him a half smile. "You don't understand how much that means to me."

He walked her to the back door and kissed her one last time before he held it open for her to enter. "How about a barbecue tomorrow at my house? Nothing special, just hotdogs and chips."

She licked her lips and nodded. "That sounds amazing."

"I've got the day shift, but I'll be home by five. Dinner will be ready by six." He leaned in for another quick kiss. He couldn't get enough of her. "I'm a phone call away." They exchanged numbers before he stepped away.

"Good night, Aiden."

He loved the way his name whispered from her lips.

"Good night, Marina."

He waited for her to close and lock the door. As he walked away, his anger toward Craig Caswell grew. That whole family was a problem. He understood how Marina had been caught in their world. They were black widow spiders waiting for someone to get tangled in their web. Craig had used his daughter as bait to lure in Marina. Once she was there, she'd been good and trapped.

Aiden's aim was to make sure they didn't get close enough to bite ever again. He turned and gave her home one last glance before he cleared the fence and went back to his deck.

Marina was special. She was vulnerable and scared, but she was his. He'd known it the minute he saw her. Confirmed it the second they kissed. He'd never put a wish on the wall before but was happy his for a kiss had been granted so quickly.

CHAPTER THIRTEEN

Marina woke to the sound of her phone. She hated to look at the screen. If it was a Caswell, she'd die. All night long she'd dreamed of Aiden and his kisses, and she didn't want the memory of that dream erased by an unwelcome call. By the third ring, she knew she couldn't ignore whoever was on the line. She lifted her phone to see it was Katie.

"Hey," she said, sounding relieved and more awake than she felt.

"Are you still in bed? It's after seven. You've got a four-year-old."

"She likes to sleep until eight." Marina wiped the sleep from her eyes and sat up.

"I'd hate you if I didn't like you so much." In the background, the whir of the mixer's bowl filled the silence. "Hold on a second. Have to add the walnuts." The pinging sound of nuts hitting the blade added a cadence to the whine. It was almost like music. "I'm back." Katie sounded out of breath. "I need you here now, as in five minutes ago."

Marina hopped out of bed, looking for the jeans she'd worn yesterday. She tugged them on. "Are you okay?"

"Yes, but this is super important, and you and Kellyn need to come right away."

"You're scaring me." What could be important enough to need her at the crack of dawn?

Katie laughed. "That's my superpower. Ask Bowie." Marina knew about Katie's heart transplant and how she took risks that scared the hell out of her family, but Katie told her if there was no risk, there was no reward. Her daughter Sahara was her biggest risk and her greatest reward.

Marina knew exactly how she felt. She'd risked everything for Kellyn and would do it again. Some things were worth putting it all on the line for. She thought about Aiden and smiled. He was another risk that seemed more like a reward.

"What's going on?" She put her phone on speaker and finished dressing. Once she'd slipped on shoes, she picked up her phone and rushed to Kellyn's room. "Tell me something. She'll be grumpy if I wake her up early, so there better be at least a muffin in it for her."

"Get over here. It's a good thing, and it'll be worth getting up early for. I promise." Katie hung up before Marina could say another word.

She shook Kellyn gently until she stirred. "Hey, sweetie. We have to get up."

Kellyn's eyes popped open. She searched the room for danger. "Nothing's wrong." God, she hoped that was true. Katie sounded excited and buoyant. She'd said it was a good thing, but Marina knew what was good could be open for interpretation. "Ms. Bishop wants us to come to the bakery. Sounds like she has a surprise for us. At least I know she has a muffin."

Kellyn rolled out of bed, dragging her doll with her. While she visited the little girl's room, Marina picked out shorts and a shirt.

"Aiden invited us over for hotdogs tonight. That will be fun, right?" Kellyn peeked around the corner, but she couldn't hide her smile. She liked Aiden, and that made Marina feel all the better about him. She might not be able to trust her gut, but Kellyn was a good judge of character. She was a tough sell, but if she liked you, it meant you were a good person.

In fifteen minutes, they were out the door and on their way to the bakery. They walked inside to find Doc Parker and his girlfriend, Agatha, sitting at the front table.

"You're here," Katie sang from behind the counter. She shoved two muffins on a plate and grabbed a chocolate milk for Kellyn on her way around the display case. Rather than put everything on an unoccupied table, she placed their plate of muffins and Kellyn's milk on the occupied table.

"Sorry, Doc," Marina said.

She reached for the plate of muffins, but Doc stopped her from picking them up. "Join us."

"Yes," Katie said with triumph in her voice. "Join them." She turned and walked into the back room, leaving the four of them alone.

"How's the house been treating you?"

She'd rented the house from Doc Parker. It had been his home before his wife passed away and his daughter left town.

"It's great. We've been working in the back-yard." She laughed. "Actually, Aiden has been working in the backyard. He planted us a garden and put in a swing for Kellyn."

They all looked down at the little one, who was busy picking the nuts out of her muffin.

"Sheriff Cooper is a good man. I'm glad he's your neighbor," Agatha said. "A woman could do worse than have a handsome lawman living next door."

Doc shook his head. "Should I worry about you and Sheriff Cooper, Agatha?" The smile on his face said he was teasing, and Lord knew Aiden was a good thirty years younger if not more, but Agatha was old and not dead. She recognized quality when she saw it.

"Oh, fiddlesticks," she said, slapping his arm. "I've got you. Why would I want Aiden?" She picked up her coffee and sipped. "Besides, I hear he has his eyes set on a little girl with brown hair. Seems to think her mother is okay too."

Marina blushed. "He's been kind to us." She looked around the room. Surely, Katie hadn't called her at the crack of dawn on a Sunday to have muffins with Doc Parker and Agatha. "Is there a reason I'm here?"

Doc took off his glasses and wiped them on his shirt before he balanced them back on the bridge of his nose. "I hear things are a bit tight for you?"

Her stomach dropped to the checkerboard floor. Was he afraid she wouldn't come up with the rent? "Yes, but I'm figuring it all out. I can assure you I'll have next month's rent. I'm no slacker, Doc Parker. I may have a last name that's synonymous with laziness and poor work ethic, but I'm a hard worker, and I'll make ends meet each month."

Doc laid his gnarled hand on top of hers. "I don't think I said I was worried about anything." He looked at Agatha. "Did you hear me say I was worried about the rent?"

She smiled. "No, dear. You said nothing about the rent."

They both stared at Marina.

"I'm confused."

Doc sat back and ran his hands through his hair. "I'm going to need a trim." He rubbed his stubbly face. "Probably a good shave too. You know how to use a straight edge?"

Marina did, but it wasn't something women requested at the beauty shop, so she was rusty. "I can give you a haircut, Doc, but I'm afraid I wouldn't trust myself with a razor close to your neck."

"That's no problem. It's a shame that a good old-fashioned shave went by the wayside years ago. Love the feel of a foamy brush on my face and the sound of a sharp blade removing my tougher-than-titanium whiskers. The older you get, the harder they hang on."

She opened Kellyn's chocolate milk. "So, I'm here because you want a haircut?"

"Yes, that's exactly why you're here. This whole damn town needs a haircut. Have you seen the Williamses' kids? Hippies, the whole lot. Then there's Tilden. He's as Grizzly Adams as they get. Lives up in the hills and helps old man Tucker make moonshine."

She'd heard about the bootleggers from Sage. "Didn't he set himself on fire?"

"Yep, Zachariah Tucker damn near killed himself." Doc looked down at Kellyn. "Excuse my language, young lady."

"Get on with it, Paul," Agatha said, using Doc's first name. "The poor girl is turning gray waiting for your offer."

"Offer?" Marina asked.

"Right. Right." He pointed across the street to the building with the whitewashed windows. "That building over yonder belongs to me. It's not fancy, but it's got the basics."

Marina's heart rate picked up. "I don't understand."

"We need a hair person. I need a cut, and while my Agatha is beautiful no matter what she looks like, she likes them rollers in her hair once a week and drives to Copper Creek to get it done. That's a long way to drive when there's a qualified hairdresser in town."

She looked between the older couple and then over her shoulder at Katie, who pointed to The Wish Wall.

Holy hell, they'd done it again. "You want me to work in your shop?"

Doc shook his head. "Nope. I don't want to own a beauty shop. Have you seen me lately? What do I know about beauty except how to admire it?" He gave Agatha a soft look, then turned his attention to Marina. "I hoped you could do me a favor and take the shop off my hands."

"Take it off your hands?"

He gave her a flustered look. "Do you always repeat what people say to you?"

"No, not usually." She wasn't sure what was going on here. Just the other day, she'd put her wish to have clients on the wall, and now she was being offered a shop. "I can't afford to buy or rent the shop."

"There she goes again, Agatha. She's hearing words I'm not speaking."

Agatha set her hand on top of Doc Parker's, whose hand was still on top of Marina's. Kellyn looked at the stack of hands and put hers on top of them like they were playing a game, but this wasn't a game. Doc Parker and Agatha were offering her the opportunity of a lifetime. "What are the terms?"

They took their hands back. Kellyn went back to her muffin while the three adults stared at the abandoned storefront across the street.

"You want terms?" Doc rubbed his whiskers. "I'll give you terms. The place is in a state. Needs a good cleaning. Probably a coat of paint too. I don't paint. It's got two sinks and three chairs. Old as dirt, but still functional. You open the doors, and people will come."

"Surely you want something for the use of the building." Nothing in her life had ever come this easy. Not that being beat for two years was easy, but being in Aspen Cove could never be considered hard.

"I thought I made that clear. I want a haircut, and Agatha wants curlers."

"Why would you do that for me?"

He gave her a fatherly smile. "Haven't you learned anything since you've been here? Aspen Cove takes care of its own. You belong to Aspen Cove. We're here for you." He took a set of keys from his pocket and set them on the table. "I get to be your first customer." He stood and offered his hand to Agatha. "You ready, lovey? I need more than a muffin on Sunday. Let's go to the diner and get bacon and eggs."

They left Marina sitting at the table staring at the keys in her hand. Seconds later, Katie plopped into Doc's vacated seat with two cups of coffee.

"Drink up. You're going to need it." She looked at her watch. "Help is coming in an hour."

"What? What help?"

Katie cupped her cheek. "Oh, honey. You'll learn."

It didn't take an hour for people to show up.

Cannon and Bowie came first with ladders and brooms. Sage arrived next with paint and brushes. As the morning faded, half the town was inside her new shop cleaning it up.

More than once, she had to excuse herself to cry. Never in her life had anyone given her so much.

At lunchtime, Maisey brought a tray of pasta for anyone who was hungry. By the time five o'clock rolled around, what once had been an abandoned beauty shop was a thing of beauty. The sinks shone like polished porcelain. The checkerboard floors sparkled as if they were new. A fresh coat of off-white paint did wonders for the yellowing walls. The old name was scraped off the window, and Cove Cuts was painted in its place. Kellyn helped too. On the wall by the front door, she painted a smiling face and a ladybug. Nothing ever looked sweeter.

The only person she hadn't seen was Aiden, but she knew he was working. Occasionally, she caught herself staring at the sheriff's office across the street, hoping to catch sight of him.

"Do you care if I steal the little sprout here for a bit?" Katie asked. "My Sahara loves her and needs some Kellyn time." Katie winked at her twice before she tossed her head toward where Aiden stood in the doorway. Katie was working her magic again.

Marina dropped to her knees. "Do you want to visit Sahara or stay here and finish up with Mommy?"

There was no hesitation. She wrapped her hand in Katie's and pulled her to the door. When she saw Aiden, she let go of Katie and raced to him. For a second, she stood in front of him as if she wasn't sure what she'd do, and then she pulled him down to her level and gave him a hug.

Marina swore the man almost cried. He hugged her back and wiped his eyes. "Lots of dust in the air."

"Whatever." Katie gave him a knowing look. "We've got Kellyn." She smiled at Aiden and then at Marina. "You kids be good."

Within minutes, everyone had cleared out of the beauty shop.

"I heard we got a hot hairstylist in town, but damn." He moved to her and took her in his arms.

CHAPTER FOURTEEN

"I'm a sweaty mess," Marina said, but she was the most beautiful woman he'd ever seen. He'd watched all day as the townsfolk came and went. Each person brought their bit of magic to Marina's world.

He'd stayed away because she needed to fully understand that she was part of a community. He would have loved to keep her to himself, but that wasn't how these things worked. Life in a small town was give and take. In Aspen Cove, it was more give than anything else. That's what he loved about the place.

With her in his arms, he pressed his lips to hers for a quick kiss. "Yes, but you're a beautiful mess."

"I'm so glad you're blind with no sense of smell."

"Baby, you smell like coconut and feel like heaven." He brushed away the hair that fell over her face. "So damn beautiful." He looked around the shop. He'd never been here when it was open. It had been vacant for a long time before he became the sheriff of Aspen Cove. He was surprised at how fresh and new it looked. "You got everything you need?"

She scanned the room. "Almost. I need to get good shampoo and other hair products, and then I'll be set."

"Hold that thought." He rushed out the door and picked up the box he'd placed there on his way inside. "Samantha called in a favor. Said she owed you. Anyway, she had these delivered from a spa in Silver Springs." He put the cardboard box down and opened it. Inside were no less than a dozen jumbo bottles of shampoo and conditioner.

"Oh my God, what's with you people?"

"It's a disease. One you caught long before you moved here. It's why you fit right in. Give me a tour?"

She held his hand and walked him around the room, pointing out where she'd wash and cut and perm and curl. Once she finished, he helped her stock the empty shelves with shampoo.

He opened a bottle and took a sniff. "Thank goodness."

She pulled it from his hand. "Does it smell good?"

"Not as good as you. If everyone around town smelled like coconuts, I'd be in trouble." He looked down at the already growing bulge in his pants.

She followed his line of sight. "Coconut does it for you, huh?"

He pulled her into his arms. "You do it for me. Shall we get to those hotdogs?"

"I should go shower first."

"I'd rather you came to my place."

"Persistent much?" She picked up her purse and walked to the door. She looked over her shoulder and smiled. "I can't believe this happened."

He stepped outside the door while she locked up the shop.

He glanced toward the once whitewashed windows. "Wishes are powerful things. I got mine when you kissed me. You got yours today."

She climbed inside her SUV, and he followed her home in the cruiser. Aiden was hyper-vigilant now that Craig had reached out to her. His eyes scanned the streets for cars that didn't belong. He didn't like that the asshole knew where to find her, but he understood why Marina had answered the phone. People like the Caswells never stopped. She had to learn to pick and choose her battles, and

Craig Caswell would be the loser if he battled with Marina.

She parked in front of her house and got out of her SUV. "Are you sure I can't take a few minutes to shower?"

While he didn't want to give up a second with her, he knew she'd feel more comfortable if she didn't feel grimy. "You go shower. I'll meet you in my backyard when you're finished."

She raced for her front door. He waited to make sure she was safely locked inside before he entered his home. Making sure she was secure comforted him.

Aiden rushed around the kitchen to get things ready. He only had hotdogs and beer, but after the kisses they shared, he was certain the food didn't matter. It was the company that counted, and for some reason, she liked his.

Smoke rose from the grill as the hotdogs split and hissed, dripping oil and juice onto the flames. He turned them and looked at the beautiful woman approaching. She'd changed into shorts, and damn those legs were amazing.

She pointed to the gate on the side of the house. He never used it because he preferred to simply hop over. It got him to where he wanted to be faster.

She exited her side gate and entered his yard, moving toward him with such grace.

"Feel better?"

"Much. Thanks for being so flexible." Her eyes left him and looked at the deck.

"Hey, while I didn't want to waste a single second of us time, you don't need my okay to do what you want."

Her chin lifted along with her smile. "Old habits." She shrugged.

He took the perfectly charred dogs off the grill just as a crack of thunder shook the house. A few drops of rain fell from the sky.

Summer storms in Colorado could be brutal with torrential rains and hail the size of baseballs. "Looks like we're eating inside." He picked up the plate of hotdogs and his beer and led her into his house.

She stopped as she entered the door. "Wow. Your place is great."

He tried to see it from her perspective. He'd spent the first year renovating everything. While hers was still stuck in the eighties, his had most of the bells and whistles people would expect in a modern home.

"It's the same as yours, only refurbished, and I think I have an extra room."

She walked into the kitchen and ran her fingers across the granite counters. "It's magnificent. I love how you take care of what you have. Your pride in ownership shows in everything you do."

He put the plate on the table next to the bag of buns. "Anything worth keeping is worth putting in the time and effort it takes to care for it, be it a house or a relationship or something else." He hoped she got the message loud and clear that she was worth keeping.

A bolt of lightning arced across the sky, followed by the boom of thunder.

"That's close." She walked to the window as the few drops of water turned into a downpour.

He thought about Kellyn. "Is Kellyn afraid of storms?" Maybe they should get her from Katie's.

"No, she likes to watch them, but if you don't mind, I'll give Katie a call just in case."

He plated up a few hotdogs and grabbed a bag of chips, then pointed to the living room while she made her call.

She came in a moment later.

"Everything okay? I'm happy to get her if she wants to come home."

Marina plopped down on the leather sofa beside him and took a plate from his hands. "Nope. She's fine. They're finger painting."

"It's just us then."

She turned to face him. "Yep, just us. Tell me, how does a man like you stay single?"

He ate a bite of his hotdog and considered his answer. If he expected her to share her story, then he had to share his. "I'm picky. Turns out I prefer single moms who cut hair."

She giggled. "You should set your standards higher."

"My standards are just fine. How's the hotdog?"

She readied the second one on her plate. "So good. I was starving."

"Are you excited about the shop?"

She swallowed her bite and nodded, picking up her beer to wash it all down. "Oh my God, I never imagined my life could be like this."

"It's just the beginning. What made you choose Aspen Cove?" It was only forty minutes from her ex. While he knew the Caswells had put restrictions on her, she could get lost more easily in a larger town.

"It's really for Kellyn. I didn't want to change too much too soon. Besides, Aspen Cove is special to me. It's the first place I ran to after..."

She didn't need to say the words. "You don't have to tell me," Aiden said.

"I want you to know everything."

She told him how on her wedding night, Craig had abused her. She'd left, and the first place she came upon was Aspen Cove. She'd stayed at the bed and breakfast.

"Where was Kellyn? Was she in the house?"

She shook her head. "Kellyn was at her grand-parents' house. It was our wedding night. That was their gift. That was my first clue. If I came home from anywhere and Kellyn was gone, or if I were home and someone came for her, I knew what the rest of the day would look like."

It gutted him to hear her story. "You wouldn't leave her."

"How could I? Her own mother left her. I couldn't be the next person to abandon her."

"He could have killed you."

She looked off into space like she remembered a moment in time. "He almost did. That's when I knew I needed a plan B."

"The blackmail?"

She sat up. "No. That came later. I learned to fight back. He monitored everything but Kellyn's appointments. He hated that she needed help. He didn't want to know about her doctor's appoint-ments. Somehow not acknowledging them made the problem go away."

"She's using silence as a coping mechanism," Aiden said.

"He hurt her. Her psychologist says she suffers from PTSD. Trauma caused her not to speak be-cause she used to, and I know it has to do with her mother. She had to see him do something to her mom. It's why Kari left and why he sent Kellyn away before he got violent."

"How generous of him," he said sarcastically. "If I was a crooked cop, I'd take him out into the woods and shoot him."

She set her empty plate on the coffee table. "You're not, and that's part of the reason why I like you. You have a solid moral compass. What man would ask if Kellyn was afraid of storms? None that I know of, only you."

His mind raced back to one statement she'd made. "You said you learned to fight back?"

"Yes. There was a woman's empowerment class next to the doctor's office. While Kellyn was in her appointment, the owner taught me some self-defense moves. Hell, for a while, I was more bruised from class than I was from Craig."

"Did you get to use it?"

"I got a hit or two in."

"Should I be afraid?" he teased.

"Only if you don't give me some of those kisses pretty soon." She looked at her watch. "I've got about an hour before I need to get Kellyn home and ready for bed."

"Come here, you." He lifted her from the cushion and placed her in his lap. His hands trailed over every appropriate-to-touch inch of her body before he laid down and pulled her on top of him.

Damn, if that didn't feel perfect, but when her lips touched his, it got better.

Inching his hand lower, he cupped her bottom and waited for her to respond. What he got was a low throaty moan that said *full speed ahead.*

When she reached under his shirt, he relaxed. She pulled and tugged until she had it off him and tossed on the floor. She sat up, straddling his hips, and looked at his body.

"You are so…" Her fingertips traced over the muscles of his chest. His skin tightened and tingled under her touch.

"So what?" He wanted her to complete her thought.

"Amazing." She ran the soft pads of her fingers over his scar. "Was it terrible?"

He moved up her waist to her breasts, where his thumbs brushed the sides. "Wanting you and not having you hurts worse."

Her body went still. "Aiden…"

"It's okay. It's not time yet. Too soon."

"No. I don't have a set time. It feels right, but…"

"It's not time. We'll know when it's time. For now, this is enough." He pulled her down and kissed her again. "When I make love to you, I want it to be perfect."

CHAPTER FIFTEEN

Marina opened the door to the shop the next morning at nine. She'd brought a box of toys for Kellyn to play with while she tended to whoever arrived for a cut.

As promised, Doc Parker was her first customer. She trimmed his hair and gave him a hug. When he tried to pay her, she refused, so he left a twenty on the counter and said it was a tip.

It was as if he'd called the next person on some imaginary list. In came Tilden Cool, who indeed looked like a mountain man who hadn't seen a set of clippers in years. Marina trimmed his beard and cropped his hair close to his head. When she finished, he looked half-human.

She decided she'd work on a donation basis.

Those who could afford more would pay more, and those who couldn't would get a good cut for what they could spare.

The shop stayed steady all morning, giving her little time to think about Aiden and his words. But when she got a lull, the only thing she thought about was him telling her when he made love to her, it would be perfect. *Perfect* was a nebulous concept, but her entire body tingled thinking about what that looked like to him.

So far, everything about him was mind-blowing. He was attentive and sweet and kind. Kellyn was half in love with him, and if Marina was honest with herself, she was too.

The bell above the door chimed, and a stranger entered. It wasn't odd to see an unfamiliar face because in the summer, Aspen Cove had a thriving tourist trade with water sports and fishing. This man, dressed in a suit and expensive Italian loafers, didn't look like a tourist. Marina knew what expensive looked like. The Caswells didn't skimp on anything when it came to their image, and neither did this man.

Kellyn took him in with caution. She'd been leaving her colored blocks at home but brought them today as if she somehow knew something was coming her way.

She pulled a yellow block out and set it on the floor beside her. Warning.

"May I help you?"

The man looked around the shop. "Just passing through. Thought I'd stop in for a trim."

Marina would have loved to tell him she was booked, but the empty shop told the truth. She didn't have the liberty of turning a paying customer away. "Sure. You want it washed or just a trim?"

"Just a trim." He pulled off his suit jacket and folded it neatly, draping it over the spare chair.

"Not from here, are you?"

He sat in her chair. She pumped the foot lever to raise him up.

"No, just checking things out for a client."

Maybe he was in real estate. "What do you do, Mr...," she asked.

He smiled while she pulled her scissors from the drawer. "I'm the owner of an asset management team."

She pulled his hair up and cut. "Oh, what type of assets?"

"More of a personal nature."

She thought that odd but shrugged and quickly finished the cut. The man creeped her out, and she wanted him gone.

"What do I owe you?" he asked.

She pointed to the jar by the register that said donations. "It's a pay-what-you-can-afford place."

"Interesting. I'd think a woman like you—" he looked at Kellyn, who hadn't taken her eyes off him, "—would need the money."

She was taken aback. "A woman like me? What does that mean?"

He leaned forward. "How hard was the fall from riches to rags?"

She stepped back. Kellyn saw her abrupt movement and fumbled for her red block.

"I don't know who you are, but you need to leave." She pointed to the door.

The man picked up his jacket. "I'm Jack, and I work for Craig. He wanted to make sure his assets were okay." The man glanced over his shoulder to where Kellyn cowered in the corner. "Ready to go home yet? This isn't really a life, Marina. It's an existence."

"Out. Get out before I force you out myself," she hissed.

He lifted his hands in surrender. "I heard you have a powerful left hook."

She pushed him toward the door. "It's nothing like my right. You want to test it out?" She fisted up and stood in the doorway, waiting for him to make a move. If he even flinched, she'd let loose on him like a raging storm. "Tell the asshole intimidation won't work."

"See ya later," he said as he strolled out of the shop.

She watched until he was out of sight before she rushed over to Kellyn. "It's okay, sweetie. We're okay. I told you there are good people and bad people in the world." She looked down at the red block gripped in her daughter's hand. "You are such a good judge of character. Aiden told me to trust my gut, but I think yours is smarter."

Marina sat on the floor and cradled Kellyn in her arms until all the tension left her body. She pulled the red block from Kellyn's hand. "How about we close up and visit Aiden?"

It broke Marina's heart to see her baby swipe up the colored blocks before she'd leave. She cradled them in her arms on the way to the sheriff's office.

When they entered, Aiden was sitting behind his desk. In front of him were a pretty young woman and a handsome young man. Marina had seen them around town, but she didn't know them by name.

As soon as Aiden saw her, he stood. "Poppy, this is Marina. She runs the beauty shop, and she's my neighbor."

They said hello and looked down at Kellyn.

Marina knew what Aiden saw first. He saw the

blocks in her hands, and his eyes went straight to hers, asking without using words. She shook her head. Craig hadn't come—in person, anyway.

Aiden strode toward Kellyn and swooped her into his arms. "And this little peanut is Kellyn."

Marina stepped forward to offer a shake to the girl first. "Nice to meet you."

Aiden interrupted. "My bad manners. This is Lloyd Dawson's daughter. She helps at the office, filing and answering phones and stuff. She came to get her first paycheck." Without letting Kellyn down, he walked her to the door. "See you next week."

He returned to his chair. Once he was seated with Kellyn in his lap, he opened his drawer to show her his candy stash. "Pick anything you want." He turned to his deputy. "Can you keep an eye on this little sprout for a second? I want to show her mom something. Kellyn gets to be the sheriff while I'm gone." Aiden took his hat from the filing cabinet and put it on her head. He squatted down in front of her. "I'll be right back. Don't go anywhere. Only one candy. Otherwise, your mom might not be happy with me."

He led Marina back to where the cells stood empty and waiting. He set his hand gently on her shoulders. "What happened?"

She didn't want to cause alarm. She also didn't

want to be a problem for Aiden. If he saw her as a chore, he might not be so inclined to spend time with Kellyn and her, and she'd miss him. She hated to admit that she needed a man in her life, but she desperately needed Aiden. He brought a calm to her existence she hadn't felt in years. "Nothing. Everything is all right."

He dropped his hands and leaned his shoulder against the bars of a cell. "It's not all right. She has those damn blocks in her hands. She hasn't had them for days."

"You're right. She hasn't, but I brought them." It wasn't really a lie. She'd carried her bag to the car even though Kellyn had packed it. "She's in a new environment, and I want her to feel safe and have a way to tell me when she doesn't."

His body seemed to relax. "Are you sure?"

She moved toward him. "Yes, Aiden. She'll be fine."

"So, nothing happened?"

She didn't want to lie to him. "All that happened was a man we didn't recognize came in for a trim. She's apprehensive about strange men."

He narrowed his eyes. "Did he do anything to you?"

"No, he got a haircut and left." That was the truth. The asshole hadn't even paid.

"Okay, but you know you can tell me if

someone bothers you."

She looked around to make sure no one was looking and gave him a quick kiss. "Yes, I know, but you can't fight my battles for me."

He turned them around and pressed her to the bars. "The hell I can't. Isn't it time someone fought for you instead of fought you?" His brows rose high enough to touch the sweep of his hair.

"Just kiss me, and then I have to go back to the shop."

All thoughts of threats and Craig melted away when his lips touched hers. His hand sat on her hips, then fell to caress her bottom. She never liked feeling trapped, but pinned between Aiden and the cell was divine. The kiss ended too soon.

"You know I care about you. I'm here if you need me."

"I know. That's why I came across the street. I needed you." She gave him a devilish smile. "Or at least your kisses."

He pushed his body close to her. "You said kisses as in plural." He tilted his head and kissed her again. "That should last you for a few."

He walked her into the front office where Kellyn sat at his desk, hat still on top of her head and a handful of melted chocolates in her palm.

"See what you did." Marina shook her head.

Aiden took a Kleenex from the box on his desk

and wiped the chocolate from her face. "I didn't think it was possible, but I made her sweeter." Once he had her cleaned up, he lifted her into his arms. He turned to Mark. "I'm going to take my girls across the street. Hold down the fort."

"No problem, boss." The young deputy smiled. "I'll be seeing you later, Marina. I'm told I need a haircut." He looked at Kellyn. "Bye, squirt. It was nice working with you."

Kellyn turned, so she was looking over Aiden's shoulder. As they walked out the door, she waved to Mark.

Marina breathed a sigh of relief. There was no telling how far that visit could have taken Kellyn back, but going over to see Aiden was the magic elixir. When they got back to the shop, Kellyn pulled out her crayons and colored. The picture was rudimentary at best, but Marina could recognize the garden, Kellyn's flowers, and Aiden standing as a tall stick figure watching over her like a protector.

Anyone who saw her daughter as damaged was stupid.

The rest of the day went by in a blur as the Williamses brought in all of their children. Poor Louise was looking like she was ready to pop, but she assured Marina she had several months to go.

Hippies wasn't how she'd have described the

brood of kids that stood like steps waiting for their turn. They had their summer hair, which was long around the ears and just falling into their eyes. She was grateful for their presence because Kellyn remembered playing with them at the park, and they all fell into a silent game in the corner.

"My kids are never this quiet. Maybe I should send them here when I'm up to my ears."

Marina finished with the last Williams and set her scissors down. "They're always welcome."

Louise stared at Kellyn for a moment. "Poor little quiet thing."

Marina stood tall and proud. "Oh, don't count her out. She's resilient and smart. She's a survivor."

Louise hugged Marina. "So is her mother. You two are going to be just fine. I feel it."

Marina laughed when she looked at Louise and saw her stomach move in a ripple across her belly. "While I believe you, what you're feeling is that little one."

"This one's already making himself known."

"Boy?" Marina asked.

Louise nodded. "No one but you knows."

"Your secret is safe with me." Marina set her hand on her flat stomach and hoped that someday she'd be as blessed as Louise. She looked at the seven kids being rounded up like sheep and said to herself, *maybe not that blessed.*

CHAPTER SIXTEEN

The week passed by in a blissful blur. Aiden spent his days at the office and his evenings with Kellyn and Marina. It was downright domestic, and he loved it. They barbecued, gardened together, and played on the swing.

Kellyn had even asked him to read her a bedtime story by tugging him into her room and handing him a book. He read *Is Your Mama a Llama.* She let out a little giggle that made his heart swell, hoping soon she'd find her voice. But when he told her it was okay to use her words, her face turned ashen, and she buried herself under the blankets. He'd pushed too far, too soon. He hated that he'd taken one step forward and two back.

He despised what Craig Caswell had done to

his girls. And Aiden considered Marina and Kellyn his. He felt a deep connection to both and couldn't imagine his life without them in it.

Today he made his rounds and hoped to finish quickly because he and Marina had a date. The Williams family had invited Kellyn for a sleepover that she happily accepted with a smile and a nod.

He'd see where the night would end, but he hoped it was in his bed with Marina in his arms. He'd never pressure her, but with the way they both desperately clung to each other, it was time to bring their relationship to the next level.

First, he had to get his job done. If he was going to make the night perfect like he wanted, like he knew she'd want, he needed to get home and work some magic.

He drove down Main Street and parked in front of the new fire station. It was almost ready. Close enough that Samantha and Katie were putting together a small-town festival to celebrate the grand opening in a couple of weeks. They'd reserved a blow-up big screen and decided to have a movie night in the park right after the ribbon cutting. Aiden had every intention of taking his girls.

He laughed out loud, remembering how Bowie and Cannon suggested they show *The Towering Inferno* or *Backdraft*, but the women chose a family-friendly show. That was why women should rule the world. They almost always made better choices.

He got out of his car and walked into the building. It was solidly constructed of brick, but the way it was designed respected the architecture of the town. In a year or so, when the façade weathered, the building would look like it had been there forever.

"Hey, Coop, come on over and meet Luke, our new fire chief." Wes nodded to the man, who was at least six foot four.

"Nice to meet you, Luke. I'm Aiden Cooper. Anything you need, just ask."

Luke and Wes took him on a tour of the place. The fire station was two stories with sleeping quarters upstairs and a pole to slide down when the alarm sounded, but Luke told him the men generally used the stairs. The pole was another way to pay tribute to the town and the era in which it was built. They planned to let the kids take turns on opening day.

"We thought that having a public servant day would be a good idea," Luke said. "The day we open, we can bring out the truck, our equipment, and whatever else we can find to entertain the people who funded this amazing project. You could bring the cruiser or open the jail cells for tours."

"That's a great idea." It had been at least two

years since they'd held an open house. As the town grew, he didn't have the manpower to provide the fun stuff, but with the influx of people coming to town, they would see more tax revenue and might be able to hire another deputy.

"It's free and could be fun," Wes added.

"Free is always good," Aiden replied. "How many men are you bringing to town?"

"We're stealing a man from the three stations in Copper Creek."

Each time Aiden heard the town of Copper Creek mentioned, his muscles twitched. He was certain if Mayor Caswell had one more son, he'd have run the fire department too. Those bastards had their hands in everything. They controlled that town with an iron fist. No doubt they would let it burn if it wasn't in their best interests to save it.

He said goodbye to Wes and Luke and steered his cruiser to the next stop. The Guild Creative Center was coming along nicely. None other than Craig Caswell had held up the permits, but once they were in place, Lockhart Construction had gone to work. Samantha's recording studio was finished. Dalton's culinary school was a week from completion, and the rest of the center would be ready for tenants shortly after the fire station opened.

He stepped out of his vehicle and peeked inside

to see Noah and Ethan Lockhart working on an electrical box.

"Just stopping in to see how things are going."

"Hey, Coop," Noah said. He was the oldest of four brothers who had a constant presence in town. Looking at them made Aiden wish he wasn't an only child. He thought about Kellyn and how much she loved to play with other kids. He'd hate to see her grow up alone. He smiled to himself. If his long-term plan worked out, he'd give her a sibling or maybe two in the not-too-distant future.

"Everything going all right?" Just last week, the Lockharts had some of their tools stolen from the site.

"We're locking everything down now. Living and working in a small town makes a person get complacent," Ethan added.

Aiden scanned the building. "Crime has no address."

Noah laughed. "It did last week, and that address was here."

"Glad it's been quiet since." Aiden was certain the equipment would show up in a pawnshop in Copper Creek or Silver Springs soon. It was only a matter of time. "I gotta go."

He drove up Main Street only to see Cannon escorting a man out of his bar. By the grip he had on the man's T-shirt, there was trouble.

Aiden parked and walked to where Cannon stood outside the Brewhouse.

"Do we have a problem here?" He recognized the man from before—the guy he'd offered an orange jumpsuit to.

The idiot looked at him. "Yeah, I got a problem with this whole town," he slurred. He turned to Cannon. "He put a two-drink limit on us."

"That's about one more than you need," Aiden replied.

"What do you know? Bet you've never had a fun day in your life."

"I've got this," he said to Cannon. Aiden lifted his forearm and pressed it against the chest of the man until he was standing against the wall. "I know that you're drunk, which means you had a few before you got here. I know that if you try to climb in your car, I'm locking you up in a cell so you don't kill someone. If you so much as blink in the wrong direction, you'll find you have bigger problems in this town."

He noticed movement to his right. Marina and Kellyn were coming out of the shop, and they stopped and stared. "Hey, sweetheart," he said without missing a beat. "I'll see you tonight."

Marina smiled. "You okay? Should I get Mark?"

"No, I've got it. We were just having a discussion about life in small towns."

"Carry on." She ushered Kellyn back to the beauty shop and disappeared.

"Where were we?" He pushed off the man's chest, making him gasp for his next breath. "Oh, that's right, I was getting ready to tell you that I've met you twice and I'm not impressed. Figure it out soon, or I'll help you. There's nothing like a week or two in a cold empty cell to bring clarity and common sense to a man." He nodded toward the door. "Go get your friends and tell them you need a ride home. Hopefully one of you is sober."

The guy nearly tripped over his feet to get away. Minutes later, the four of them walked out of Bishop's Brewhouse and climbed into a beat-up pickup and drove off. Aiden wouldn't have been surprised if those were the thieves.

Cannon stood at the doorway. "Who said growth is good?"

"Not me." Before he could get delayed again, he headed for home.

THE HOUSE WAS CLEAN. He'd changed the bed and cut every flower from his garden to place around the house. He'd picked up several candles from Abby Garrett, who made them from beeswax. The bottle of wine was aerating on the counter.

The meal he'd ordered from Dalton was in the oven. The cheesy, garlicky smell of chicken parmesan filled the air.

Marina once remarked how much she liked him in light blue, so he dressed in her favorite shirt and jeans and waited.

At a quarter to six, he heard her pull up. By six, he was pacing the floors. His damn nerves were strung tight. When a light knock sounded at the front door, his heart nearly leaped from his chest.

He opened the door to find her standing there as beautiful as ever. Wearing a sundress, she looked stunning. "Beautiful. Always so beautiful."

He pulled her inside and kissed her. He loved the way she melted in his arms. It was as if his kisses weakened her knees.

When he pulled away, he looked at the heat of passion in her eyes. Dinner might have to wait.

"Did you get Kellyn to the Williamses' okay?"

"She practically dragged me there. I swear if she could drive, she would have taken my keys and left an hour ago."

"She likes the kids. She likes to play."

She pressed her head against his chest. "I like you, and I like to play too." Her hands roamed up his chest to wrap around his body before she settled them on his ass.

"You're killing me. How am I supposed to do

the right thing here with you telling me you want to play and moving your hands around my body like you want more than a kiss?" He stood back a step. "Do you want more than a kiss?"

She pulled her lower lip between her teeth and gnawed. When it popped free, it was red and puffy.

"I want you, Aiden. All of you, but I'm scared."

He tugged her back to his chest. "I'll never hurt you. All I want is to make you happy. To make you feel good."

"I want you to make me feel good." She peeked around him toward the kitchen. "How long before dinner?"

He glanced at his watch. "Thirty minutes."

She held his hand and walked him toward his room. "We've got time."

He stopped. "Oh, honey, if you think thirty minutes is enough time, you're mistaken. When I take you to my bed, you'll be there for hours."

He turned her around and walked her to the kitchen, where he poured her a glass of wine and pulled out her seat. "Have a glass of wine. Let me feed you. If you want me to make love to you, I will, but you'll need your energy because once I start, it will be a long time before I finish."

A shudder shook her body. He hoped it was from excitement and not fear.

She was on her second glass of wine when they

started dinner. They talked about their day, but all they had on their minds was each other.

She'd eaten half her meal when she laid her fork down and said, "I can't stand it anymore. Take me to bed."

A chill raced down his spine. It was half anticipation and half anxiety. What if he didn't satisfy her? What if he fell short of everything she imagined their first time would be?

"You got it." With the confidence he wasn't sure he had, he swept her into his arms. Carrying her into his room, he placed her on top of the navy-blue bedspread where he had imagined her many times, but his mind couldn't conjure how incredible the actual experience could be. "Let me set the mood."

He lit the candles he'd placed around the room, and their honeyed scent floated through the air as they burned. Then he sat on the edge of the bed next to her.

"Are you sure you want to do this?" He hated to ask because it gave her the option to change her mind, but it was important to him that she went into the night understanding what it meant to him.

"I'm sure."

He kicked off his shoes and lay down beside her. His hand fell to her hip while his forehead pressed against hers. "This isn't just sex for me. I'm falling in love with you, Marina. When our bodies connect, you become mine in my heart and my mind."

She toed off her shoes, and they hit the floor with a thud. Her eyes stayed locked on his.

Tilting her chin so their lips met, he took her mouth in a long, lazy kiss that seemed to last for minutes. She tasted sweet with a hint of wine. His hunger couldn't be sated with a single kiss. Each moan and whimper that slipped from her beautiful mouth caused a craving inside that drove him forward. He wanted more. He needed more.

He trailed his hand from her hip to the zipper at the back of her dress. Slowly he lowered it tooth by tooth until the yellow material fell from her shoulder to show a pink lace bra beneath. She lifted her hips so he could pull the fabric away and toss it aside.

"Your turn," she said breathlessly while she tugged at the hem of his T-shirt until it rode high on his chest.

"Wait." He covered her hands with his. "I want to look at you. Really look at you." He leaned back and took her in from the top of her head to her pink-painted toenails. She was perfection. The need in her eyes called to him. "Do you have any idea what you do to me?" Her pale skin nearly glowed against his dark bedspread.

She briefly glanced down to his pants. "I've got a good notion."

A minute later, he was shirtless, and it was her turn to devour him with her eyes.

"You're so beautiful," she said as she traced her fingers over his chest, down his stomach to the button of his jeans.

"That's something I've never been called." Few men thought of themselves as beautiful, but he believed that she thought he was. He saw the conviction in her eyes. Her expressive eyes didn't lie.

He kissed her lips, jaw, and neck, then made his way to her breasts. He teased her aroused nipples through the pretty lace. She pressed forward into him like she was offering him more—needed more.

He nibbled her over the material until it was damp, and her breath was labored. With skillful hands, he reached behind her to unsnap and discard the lacy fabric. Ripe breasts heaved under his lips. He lavished them equally before he left a wet trail of kisses down her stomach to the edge of her matching panties. It didn't take him long to remove them and find pleasure in her sweet taste.

It was his plan to indulge for minutes or maybe hours if need be. Her pent-up passion burst forth. He didn't expect her to teeter on the edge of her release so quickly. She moved beneath his mouth, sometimes pulling him in and at others pushing him away.

"Oh...oh...Aiden," she said in a sexy, breathy exhale. "It's been so long. So damn long."

He pulled the swollen nub into his mouth until her legs shook, her breath hitched, and a moan of pure satisfaction filled the air.

What a beautiful sight it was to have this woman come undone in his arms. When he was sure he'd drawn every quiver from her body, he moved up to kiss her mouth.

He shifted to stand so he could shed his jeans. She pressed against him, clinging to him like she feared he would leave.

"I'm here. I'm not going anywhere."

"You have no idea how amazing that was." A single tear ran down her face.

By her smile, he knew it wasn't caused by sorrow.

He brushed it away. "Amazing for *me* to know I can please you. All I want is to make you happy." He cupped her face in his palm. "You want to rest, or do you want more?" He prayed she wanted more. His length throbbed with need. He didn't want to wait another minute to be inside her, but he would if that was what she needed. Without a doubt, she'd be worth the wait.

She lifted on her elbow, the flush of passion coloring her skin. Pink splotches laid a path where he'd licked and kissed her body from her neck to her core.

"Let me love you," she said, reaching for him.

"Baby, let's love each other." He opened his nightstand drawer, pulled out a condom, and rolled it on before he found his place between her thighs. "Look at me," he said as he pressed against her. "I want you to see me when I make love to you. See the man I am. A man who worships you."

He pressed inside and watched her eyes grow heavy with desire. Inch by inch he filled her until there was no place else to go. Being one with Marina was almost more than he could take. Never had he felt so complete as he did in that moment.

Looking deep into her eyes, he made promises he would always keep. "I will never hurt you." He pulled back and pressed forward. "I'll always give you more than I take." In and out he moved, pulling her body to the edge again. "You're beautiful." Again and again, he thrust inside her. "You are worthy." She moved with him, but her eyes never left his. He saw her desire, but most importantly, he saw her love. "I want you to be mine."

She cried out, "Yours."

She rotated her hips against him, her pulsing heat pulling him in. He wanted this to last forever, but he knew their first time was almost over. Energy vibrated through their bodies. She tumbled off the precipice of passion with his name on her lips.

Aiden couldn't hold out any longer. His body stilled as he reached the height of his pleasure. She tugged him deeper, and he let it all go. He knew his life had changed. He was undeniably in love with Marina.

He pulled her close and traced hearts on her hip. He wanted her to know exactly how he felt. It was a make-or-break moment, but he had to say what was in his heart. "I know it's soon," he said. "But...I love you—everything about you. I love Kellyn too."

She curled into him like she couldn't get close enough. "You know what's crazy? I love you too, Aiden. I'd promised myself I'd never let another man into my heart, but you moved in, and it feels so right."

He gave her a languid kiss. One that said he was in this for the long haul. He knew in his heart they made sense. Everything about them was right.

They made love one more time before they fell asleep in each other's arms.

CHAPTER SEVENTEEN

Waking up to Aiden was pure heaven. Who would have thought that she would allow a man into her heart and bed? Well, his bed technically.

He set a cup of coffee on the nightstand. "This is for you. I picked up muffins yesterday, so there are a few on a plate in the kitchen. I wish I could have made you breakfast, but it was get up early or stay lying next to you. I was selfish and chose you."

She rose up and pulled the sheet to cover her breasts before she reached for the coffee. "You're too good to me. Thank you." Wasn't the morning after supposed to feel awkward? She lay in Aiden's bed, and dammit if it didn't feel almost perfect. Perfect would have been if he'd been naked next to her. She pressed her thighs together and felt the delicious tenderness that came after a night of making love.

He stared at her with longing. "As much as I hate to leave you, I've got to go to work." He leaned over and kissed her. "What are you doing today?"

She'd closed the shop today because Kellyn had to go to therapy. "I'll be in Copper Creek most of the day."

Aiden narrowed his eyes. "That's right. Kellyn's appointment." He laid his hand on her sheet-covered thigh. "Be careful."

She could see the worry in his eyes. "It'll be fine. We're going to her doctor's appointment, and then I usually take her to the burger place with the big ball pit. She likes to play there."

"I'm only a phone call away. If there's any sign of trouble, I want you to call me."

She didn't expect trouble, but she hadn't expected an uninvited visit from Craig's spy at the shop either. That was the problem with Craig, he was unpredictable, but she refused to live in fear.

"I'll be fine. We'll be fine."

"Okay, how about dinner here tonight?"

Marina smiled at him. "How about dinner at our house? I'll cook since you're working."

He bent over and gave her a kiss she'd remember all day. "That sounds like a deal." He stood and looked down at her. "How am I supposed to sleep without you tonight? One night and I'm hooked." He shook his head. "Whoever said kids were the best form of birth control had it right."

"We'll figure it out. You know they say absence makes the heart grow fonder."

He mussed her hair. "You can't get more fond than in love." He stepped away and smiled. "I'll see you tonight. Don't hurry to leave. The shower is great. Everything I have is yours."

She slipped out of bed and walked to him to give him one last kiss. "I'll miss you too."

He let his eyes linger over her body. "Damn, I'm an idiot for not taking the day off."

She laid her hand over his badge. "Someone has to protect us. Go to work. I'll be home when you get home."

"I'll hurry."

She watched him walk down the hallway and listened to the door open, shut, and lock. *Was it possible for life to be so kind to her after so many years of sorrow?*

A look at the clock told her she had enough time to enjoy Aiden's shower before she had to pick up Kellyn.

An hour later, she was dressed in workout gear, knocking on Louise's door.

When she opened it, Louise smiled. "That must have been some good night. You're glowing."

Marina knew by the heat on her face she was blushing. She looked around to make sure no children were within hearing range. "Oh my God, thank you for watching Kellyn. It was a life-altering night."

Louise's eyes grew large. "Life altering?" She rested her hand on her stomach. "I'll show you life altering. It starts with one amazing night and ends eight kids later."

She invited Marina inside the house, which was neat and tidy despite the nine people who lived there.

"I don't know how you do it." She followed Louise down the hallway to a room on the right where all the girls sat in a circle dressing Barbie dolls.

"You have to have more than one. Once there are multiples, they entertain each other."

The kids looked up. Kellyn dropped her doll and came racing for Marina, who swept her into her arms and hugged her tightly.

"Did you like your sleepover?" It was the first time anyone other than her grandparents had taken her overnight. Marina would have been nervous if she hadn't gotten to know Louise through play dates at the park. Everyone in town loved her. If she could care for seven children, there was no reason she couldn't care for Kellyn.

Her daughter smiled and nodded. She opened her mouth like she was going to say something but closed it and buried her head in the crook of Marina's neck.

"She was an angel." Louise leaned in and kissed the top of her head. "Hardly knew she was here. Maybe she could come back again soon." Louise gave Marina an I've-got-your-back look.

"Would you like that, Ladybug?" Marina asked.

Kellyn nodded and squirmed out of her arms. She raced back to Louise's girls, giving them each a hug before she picked up Mrs. Beasley and returned, ready to go.

"How about Saturday?" Louise suggested.

Marina's heart raced. Could she possibly be back in Aiden's bed in three days? "I couldn't impose," she said. Inside, her brain was screaming, *Yes, Saturday is perfect.*

"Saturday it is." Louise walked them to the door. "He's a good man, and he needs a good woman like you"

A warm fuzzy filling moved through Marina's insides. "I need him more." She walked down the steps before she turned and said, "Thank you for helping to make my life whole."

THEY ENTERED Kellyn's therapist's office. Dr. Thayer smiled when she saw them.

"Hey, you," she said to Kellyn. "Are you ready to play?" She glanced at Marina. "She looks calm and happy."

That statement was true. She had a peacefulness about her that had been missing. "She is happy." Kellyn raced to the Lego table while Marina caught Dr. Thayer up on everything that had happened since their last visit a month ago.

"So, she's settled in, and there's a new man in your life. She has friends. I'm so glad things are working out. Has she talked?"

With a shake of her head, Marina said, "No, but she's giggled out loud. I swear I hear her whispering to Mrs. Beasley. I'm kind of jealous of the damn doll."

"She's testing the waters. The safer she feels, the quicker her walls will crumble. She'll talk when she's ready and when she does, it's best if you don't make a big deal out of it. I imagine as she lets her guard down, things might slip out."

"I feel like I'm waiting for Christmas, and her first word will be the present I've been wanting my entire life to open."

"It will happen. I'm sure of it." She walked Marina to the door. "Will you be next door?"

She went to the self-defense center each time

180

Kellyn had her appointment. Dr. Thayer thought it was important for Kellyn to have no distractions.

"Yes." She looked down at her yoga pants and sneakers. "Maybe I can learn another move or two to add to my bag of tricks."

"See you in an hour."

Marina walked into the center that had taught her how to defend herself. Julie, the instructor, left the punching bag and rushed over to hug her.

"Oh my God, you look amazing." She walked around her until she'd made a full circle.

"I'm happy. Things are good. I'm feeling empowered." She remembered the first day she had arrived there, and Julie took one look at her and rushed her inside. She told the instructor she didn't have any money, but Julie gave her a hug and said that need outweighed compensation. But now, she could pay because the people of Aspen Cove had been generous with their tips the past week. Since Julie was always generous with her time in the past, Marina wanted to repay her. Pulling a hundred-dollar bill from her pocket, "It's not much, but it's something."

Julie folded her hand over Marina's. "I don't want your money. I'm just so happy you made it out alive."

"I did, but I had help." She forced the money back into the instructor's hand. "Use it for the next woman who needs support but can't afford it."

They moved to the bag, where Julie told her to warm up. As she threw a few punches and kicks, she closed her eyes and remembered that last day.

He'd come home from the office. He found her in the living room playing with Kellyn.

It made her sick to know that her baby girl saw it all. She had no warning it was coming. Usually, he had his parents pick up Kellyn. That was always the clue, but not that day.

He came in, grabbed a glass of scotch, and joined her in the living room. The scotch was her sign that all was not well. She wondered what his excuse would be today. Had she looked at the mailman seductively? Did he think she blew the gardener while Kellyn took her nap? Was there a spot on the counter? A wrinkle in his shirt? Maybe it was because it was Friday. It didn't matter; she knew it was coming, but this time she was prepared. The quicker it was over, the sooner she could move on with plan B.

She asked Kellyn to go to her room. Marina didn't want her to see what was going to happen. Kellyn looked at Craig, gathered her toys, and ran down the hallway.

Most days, Marina would fight. Not today. Not until she had what she needed. Today she'd take every push, slap, and punch because today would be the last time. She glanced at the teddy bear that sat on the shelf and smiled as the first blow came.

When it was over, Craig left, and she crawled away. Her world crashed around her when she saw Kellyn cowering in the corner. She'd witnessed it all. Marina cradled her in her arms and told her it would be okay. She promised her they would leave and never come back. That was what they did. She packed them up and took a taxi to a cheap motel outside of town. No one would think to look for her in Cross Creek. The town was a blip on the screen. Hardly noticeable at all. While she healed, she implemented plan B.

That recording had been her golden ticket out.

She didn't realize how hard she was hitting the bag until Julie pulled her back. "Feeling aggressive?"

"Just remembering."

"It's good to remember, but better to plan." Julie showed her a few new self-defenses moves before Marina was due to pick up Kellyn. "See you next month," she said as Marina walked out the door.

Kellyn was in good spirits when they arrived at the burger joint. She raced into the ball pit while Marina ordered their lunch. She noticed a familiar face at a table in the corner. Wes Covington sat with a few of the crew from The Guild Creative

Center, and they were huddled over some papers while they ate. She considered stopping by to say hi but didn't want to interrupt them, so she grabbed her tray and went back to the playroom.

Kellyn was buried beneath the balls. It was one of her favorite things to do, so Marina left her to crawl through them for a few more minutes.

The hair rose on the back of her neck. She had no time to look around when hands came to her shoulders and gave her a painful pinch. "You shouldn't hang up on your husband."

Marina stilled. She said a silent prayer that Kellyn wouldn't come out of the balls anytime soon. "You're not my husband. Our marriage was annulled. As far the court system is concerned, we were never married."

He let out a grunt. "And yet you still carry my last name."

She hated that she did. "It's easier for Kellyn's sake." She didn't want to bring up her daughter for fear that he'd seek her out, but it wasn't Kellyn he was after. He only used her as a pawn. It was revenge he wanted, and that could only be satisfied with bruises and bloodshed.

"How is the little mute?"

God, how she wanted to turn around and punch him, but she didn't dare because it would draw attention and Kellyn would see. Her best bet was to get him to leave. "She's adjusting." She'd never tell him she was thriving. "You're breaking the restraining order."

He let out a laugh that chilled her through and through. "What are you going to do, call my brother? They gave it to you because you have no way to enforce it. You can't keep me away. I'll always be around."

"Please leave us alone."

He ran his hands down her arms and squeezed her biceps until she whimpered. "I love it when you beg."

Victor, not a victim, she reminded herself. She took in a deep breath, inhaling the scent of Aiden's body wash and shampoo. He was there with her in spirit, and the presence of his scent gave her strength. She spun around to push Craig away. "You need to leave now."

He looked around. "You smell like another man. Don't forget who you belong to."

She refused to let him intimidate her. "Oh, I won't. Do you like his scent on me?" It wasn't smart to antagonize him, but she was done cowering. Craig Caswell no longer had any power over her.

His face turned cherry red. The balls in the pit behind her moved. She turned away from Craig and walked to where Kellyn popped up. Marina hoped that her body shielded her daughter from seeing him. When she turned around, relief washed over her. He was gone. The only thing that remained was the pinkish-purple marks he'd left on her arms.

"How about we take our lunch home today?" She didn't want to spend another minute in a place where Craig could get to them. He was right. As long as she was in Copper Creek, she'd never be safe. She was also stupid because the first thing she should have done was change up the schedule. He knew where she'd be the last Wednesday of every month. She might as well have sent him an invitation. His absence while at rehab had given her a false sense of security., and she'd been careless— lesson learned.

CHAPTER EIGHTEEN

Aiden was filing paperwork in the office when Lloyd Dawson walked in.

"Poppy doesn't work today," Aiden said.

"I know that," Lloyd grumbled. "I wanted a minute with your deputy."

They both looked at Mark's empty desk.

"He's out on rounds."

Lloyd pulled up a chair in front of Aiden's desk. "I don't want him around my daughter."

Taken aback, he stared at the man. Since he'd hired Poppy, Aiden knew she was well past the age of needing her father's consent. "They work in the same office. It would be impossible to avoid each other. If it's any consolation, I've never seen the two of them look at each other with more than courtesy." Aiden wasn't sure if that was the honest to God truth. He had paid little attention to the way they looked at each other, but he knew Mark liked Poppy. Having an interest and showing an interest were two different things.

Lloyd pushed to his feet and walked to the door. "Good to know." He was gone before Aiden could say another word.

He didn't get much time to think on it because Wes walked in looking concerned.

"Don't tell me there was another equipment theft at the site?" Aiden reached inside his drawer to get the forms ready for Wes to fill out. He hated there had to be so much paperwork, but that was the way of the world.

"No," Wes said and took the chair Lloyd had vacated.

"Don't tell me you've got someone you don't want my deputy dating too?"

Wes shook his head. "I wouldn't take it too kindly if he put the moves on my wife, but I don't see that happening. I'm here about something else." He looked down at his twiddling thumbs.

It was obvious something serious was bothering him. By his nervous gestures, this wasn't a social call. "What's on your mind?"

Wes looked up. "Have you talked to Marina today?"

At the mention of her name, he sat up and leaned forward. "No, she had to take Kellyn to an appointment in Copper Creek."

"Yes, I saw her there. But..."

Aiden's stomach tightened. For Wes to hem and haw over something meant he was torn about whether to say anything at all. "What happened?" The sheriff in him knew he couldn't demand an answer, but the man in him wanted one.

"Craig Caswell showed up, and whatever happened didn't look pretty."

"Did he touch her?" Fury boiled under Aiden's skin, but so did concern. He'd thought they were at a place in their relationship where she'd trust him. Just that morning, he told her to be careful and to call him if anything came up. He pulled his phone from his pocket. There wasn't a call from Marina.

"I was in the back booth, so I didn't have a good view, but he grabbed her arms." Wes smiled. "She turned on him like a lioness ready to attack. I saw the push and got up to go help, but he took off, and she got Kellyn from the ball pit and left."

Aiden was on his feet with his keys in hand. "How long ago was that?"

"About an hour."

"I've got to go." He came just short of pushing Wes out the door. He locked up and called Mark, telling him he was on call the rest of the night.

He had no idea what to expect. There was a good chance the asshole had done something far worse to her than grab her. Aiden knew words could be more powerful than actions. A victim of domestic abuse once told him the bruises healed, but the words lingered in her heart and head forever.

His career be damned. He'd kill the man if there was something wrong with Marina or Kellyn.

When he pulled into his driveway and saw his girls were home, the first thing he did was take a deep, calming breath.

He hopped out of the cruiser and went inside to change. He wanted to talk to her as Aiden her boyfriend, not Sheriff Cooper. This conversation could go one of two ways. He hoped it went his way.

Dressed in jeans and a polo shirt, he knocked on the door. A shadow crossed in front of the peephole, which meant Marina was being cautious.

She opened the door and smiled. "Hey, you're off early."

He lowered his head so she wouldn't see the truth. "We need to talk." When his eyes rose to meet hers, he saw a glimpse of fear. He realized that was the stupidest way to lead into a conversation. "Not like you're thinking."

Air whooshed from her lungs. She moved aside and let him in. "Oh, that's a relief. I thought—"

She wore yoga pants and a T-shirt covered by a hoodie. Odd for such a warm day. It told him a lot about what had gone down at lunch.

"I'm not giving you up," Aiden said. "You'll have to break my heart into a thousand pieces before I let you go, because if one sliver remains intact and beating, I will still want you."

He considered coming straight out with what he knew, but he had to trust that she'd tell him. It was one way to gauge how much confidence she had in him.

"How was your day?" she asked.

"Good. How was yours?" He looked around the sparsely furnished living room. "Where's Kellyn?"

"She's taking a nap. Between the Williamses and the ball pit, she was tuckered out."

"Did she have a good visit with the therapist?"

Marina chuckled. "How bad could playing with Legos for an hour be? She didn't bring her blocks, so that was a plus."

His jaw tensed. The one time she didn't have her blocks, and she needed them. "So, everything was okay today? No problems, no..."

She turned away from him. "Yes, everything turned out okay."

He had to give it to her. She wasn't lying to him.

She appeared okay, and if Kellyn was napping, then she was unlikely traumatized. He followed her into the kitchen, where she was preparing their dinner. On the counter sat several chicken breasts she'd been dipping in egg and dredging in flour.

"Okay. That's great." While he was disappointed she didn't tell him the truth, he had to let her work it out. "You have a kiss for me?" He stepped to her side and placed his hands on her arms, turning her to face him. The light pressure caused her to wince.

She pulled back. "I worked out at the self-defense center. I must have pulled a muscle." She rubbed her arms and leaned in to give him a quick peck on the lips.

He had two choices: he could trust that she'd tell him, which at this point he wasn't confident she would, or he could let her know in a roundabout way that he knew what had happened. He chose the latter because it ate at him that she didn't call him when she was in danger.

"I ran into Wes."

She turned around and leaned against the counter. By the surprised look in her eyes, she knew that he knew. "It wasn't a big deal," she said. "I handled it."

Aiden walked to her and removed her hoodie to show the bruises blooming on her arms. "This is a big deal to me. He touched you. He hurt you, and you didn't trust me enough to call me."

She tugged her hoodie from his hands and tossed it on a nearby chair. "It's not that I didn't trust you. I knew you'd come. I knew you'd act. I'm not willing to give you up."

He considered her statement. He drew her into his arms. "I have to be able to protect you. I told you last night, the minute we made love, things changed. While I won't pound my chest and drag you by the hair into my cave, you are mine to love and protect. How can I do that when you don't tell me things?" It took everything inside him to keep his voice calm. He knew he'd lose her if he showed frustration instead of restraint.

She tucked her head against his chest and breathed him in. "He said I smelled like a man." She placed her hand over his heart. "I used your body wash today so I could smell like you. You were with me the whole time. I stood up for myself. I pushed him away, and then I left."

"He broke the restraining order. I can do something about that."

Marina tilted her chin to look at him. "No, you can't. He knew he did it. Even he knows that a phone call to his brother won't accomplish anything."

Aiden knew it was true. "Maybe I should pay him a visit."

She fisted his shirt. "Please don't. Let it go. It's over."

That must be a lie she told herself because men like Craig didn't understand what *over* looked like. He had no intention of letting it go—letting her go. She was right that going to Chief Caswell wouldn't garner them any favor, but maybe a visit to the mayor would have merit. "I will drop it for now, but only because I want to kiss you. This isn't over. Don't try to convince me or yourself it is."

He lowered his head and took her mouth in a hungry kiss. Their tongues danced until she was breathless, and he was so hard it was painful.

When a sound came from the hallway, they broke apart, with Marina going back to her chicken breasts and Aiden taking a seat at the table so he didn't embarrass himself.

In shuffled Kellyn, dragging Mrs. Beasley behind. She fisted her tired eyes with one hand and walked straight toward him. She dropped her doll and held out her arms.

Aiden smiled at the precious one in front of him. How Craig Caswell could have had anything to do with creating something so sweet was a mystery to him.

"Pease," a whisper broke the silence.

Marina dropped the chicken breast.

Aiden lifted Kellyn to his lap. "Did you just say *please*?" he asked her.

Her eyes grew wide like she was in trouble.

"I'm so proud you used your words and manners," he said, trying not to make a big deal out of the monumental occasion that had just taken place. The first word out of her mouth had been *please*, and she had asked him to hold her. "Give me a hug." He looked over her shoulder to Marina, who was trying to contain her tears. Her mouth hung open in awe.

"How long before dinner?" Aiden asked.

She put the tray of breaded chicken into the oven. "About forty-five minutes."

He stood and held Kellyn high in the air. "How about we check on the daisies and play on the swing?" He turned toward Marina. "Is that okay with you, Mom?"

"Absolutely."

Aiden put Kellyn on her feet and tapped her bottom. "Go get your shoes, little monkey."

Kellyn took off to her room.

Marina waited for her to be out of sight before she threw herself in Aiden's arms. "Oh my God," she whispered. "Did she really say *please*?"

"I think. I'm pretty sure she wasn't asking for peas."

"I've been waiting for years." She hugged him tightly. "I'm so glad you didn't make a huge deal out of it. Dr. Thayer says she'll talk when she's ready, and I shouldn't force it. One word is more than I hoped for."

Kellyn raced around the corner with her shoes on the wrong feet.

Aiden lifted her to the table and pulled them off. "You'll be able to go faster if these are on right." Once he had them flipped around, the three of them were out the door and running to the swing, and Craig Caswell was a distant memory.

CHAPTER NINETEEN

Kellyn turned her head and waved goodbye to Marina, who had second thoughts about letting her stay the night at the Williamses'. Not because she didn't trust Kellyn would be cared for, but because she was afraid she'd miss her second word.

After that first *please*, nothing else was said.

Louise, who was getting bigger by the day, answered the door with a smile. Kellyn rushed past her without giving Marina a second glance. It should have stung, but she was so happy her little girl was finding her place in Aspen Cove.

"Come on in."

Marina stepped inside the door and stopped. Aiden was waiting for her, so she couldn't stay and visit. "Thanks for taking her."

Louise gave her a knowing smile. "She's happy here. She loves the girls, and they love her. It's like having another sister." She looked at Marina's dress and heels. "Going someplace fancy?"

"I don't know. It's a surprise. Aiden told me to dress up."

"You look beautiful. I'd be surprised if he didn't take one look at you and cancel everything."

Marina blushed. "I wouldn't be unhappy if he did." She craned her neck to look down the hall to see if she could catch a glimpse of Kellyn. "If she says anything, don't make a big deal of it, but call me right away."

Louise's eyes sparkled. "Is she talking?"

Marina tilted her head. Did a single word count? *Damn straight it did.* "Yes, she said *please* the other day when she wanted Aiden to pick her up." Marina thought Louise would turn to molten mush and collapse on the floor right there.

"He's so good for both of you."

There was no doubt about that, but the bigger question was if they were good for him. Aiden had stayed silent about Craig since Wednesday, but silence didn't mean he'd let it go. She wondered if they'd have to revisit the subject tonight. It was so hard to have candid conversations with her daughter around because saying Craig's name sent her running.

"Aiden's a good man." She remembered the first day she met him. Her first instincts were correct. Maybe she wasn't such a bad judge of character after all.

"What are you waiting for? Go get your man and have fun tonight. Your baby is safe here."

Marina hugged Louise and raced as fast as her heels would take her to her SUV.

She hadn't seen Aiden all day. He'd been at an out-of-town meeting, and when he got home, he texted her to say he was climbing into the shower and would be ready when she got back from dropping off Kellyn.

When she pulled in front of her house, he was sitting on her porch with a bouquet of roses. Her heart skipped a beat.

He stood as she approached. "You get more damn beautiful each day I see you." He handed her the flowers and gave her a kiss that promised more.

She brought them to her nose and breathed in the sweet scent. "You are way too good to me."

"Let's put these in water and get on our way. We've got reservations, and then when we get home —" he waggled his brows "—I'll be really good to you."

"We can skip dinner and go straight for the good."

"Nope. I want to show you off."

They spent a few minutes in her house putting the flowers in a mason jar, then they were in Aiden's Mustang driving toward Copper Creek.

"Where are we going?" As they neared the best steakhouse in town, her stomach felt sick. This was Caswell country, and their presence wouldn't go unnoticed.

He reached for her hand. "Who loves you?"

She sucked in a breath. "You do."

"We will not cower. You said it yourself. You're a victor, not a victim. You deserve a life and a good steak." He pulled the car into valet and handed the keys over. "Let's have dinner. We are celebrating our favorite word."

She thought of lots of words she liked when they came from Aiden. Words like *love* and *kiss* and *passion*. "What's our word?"

He opened the door and winked at her. "*Pease...* as if you'd have to ask."

How silly she was. *Pease* was the best word in the universe.

The hostess showed them to a table. Aiden pulled her chair out and took the one next to her. He ordered a bottle of wine and held her hand in his. "See, this isn't so bad." He squeezed hers for comfort.

"No." She relaxed. "This is great." It was great. She was on a real date with the man she loved. A man who cherished her, kissed her like she was the last woman on earth, and made love to her like she was everything. "Have you been here before?"

He winked at her. "Is that your way of asking if I've been here on a date?"

The waiter came with the wine and filled their glasses.

She hadn't really thought about Aiden dating anyone else, but why wouldn't he? He'd been in Aspen Cove for years. "Have you?"

"Nope. You're the first. I'd be lying to say I haven't been on a date or two, but none of them were steakhouse worthy, and none got a second date or a promise of my heart."

He always knew what to say to make her swoon.

"I bet you were quite the player in high school."

"Me?" A deep, full-bodied laugh rolled out of him. "I had braces and pimples. I also had a father who demanded I respected women. Somehow, being a player and being respectful to women wasn't a match."

She sipped her wine, and when the waiter asked for their order, they both ordered steak because what else would a person order in the best steakhouse in Copper Creek?

"Surely you dated."

"I did. I went to prom. I lost my virginity to

Roxanne Belvedere under the bleachers at home-coming. I had game."

"Roxanne Belvedere? Sounds like a porn star."

Aiden chuckled. "Nope, she was the police chief's daughter. Our fathers worked together."

"Dangerous."

"Safe really, because neither of us were talking about it, knowing if it got to our dads' ears, we'd both be doing hard time at home."

"Sounds like you already did hard time—with Roxanne." Her shoulders shook with laughter.

"Are you jealous? It sounds like you might be."

She loved the way they could tease each other. "Maybe," she said. She'd never had that with anyone else. One mention of a past relationship, and things turned dark. One thing she loved about Aiden was she could be herself. She could talk about anything without fear.

"Just remember, it's all that practice that gave me the skills to make your body sing."

"Now you're just bragging."

The waiter brought their meals.

"Eat up, sweetheart. You're going to need that big meal if I'm going to show you all my skills."

"Are you sure you want to blow your load in one night?"

While he laughed at her choice of words, she

took a bite of steak and hummed with satisfaction. It was the best steak she'd ever tasted.

They finished their meal and wine over the next hour. Marina couldn't remember a day where she felt so happy or carefree.

That all ended when a set of hands rested on her shoulders, and she saw in Aiden's eyes a murderous glare.

She turned to look up at Mayor Caswell.

"Marina, so good to see you."

She put on a fake smile and returned the nicety. "Mayor Caswell." She turned to his wife. "Mrs. Caswell, I hope you're doing well."

The mayor looked at Aiden. "Good to see you again."

Right then, she knew he hadn't let it go. She had no idea if she should be glad that he was fighting for her or angry that he'd insinuated himself into her business.

"Mayor." Aiden reached across the table and took her hand. "I ran into the mayor today and told him about your problem."

Her breath left her. She didn't know where the next one would come from. Her mouth dried, and any word she might have said was stuck in her throat.

The mayor looked her over as if searching for injury, but he'd never see them because she'd worn a three-quarter-sleeve dress that covered the bruises on her arms.

"I've taken care of it." The mayor smiled, but she knew the look. It was one of intimidation that said *we have a deal*. "It's all good now. Back to the original plan."

Marina said nothing but nodded. When they walked away, she grabbed her purse from the empty chair and ran for the door.

Aiden had to pay for dinner, so he took a few minutes to catch up. He handed the claim card to the valet attendant before he walked to her.

She spun around and yelled, "How could you? You poked the biggest bear of all. He knows I told you." She paced in front of the restaurant. Her heart beat so hard she was certain it would exit her chest any second. "I could see it in his eyes." She looked to the door to make sure the mayor wasn't standing there listening.

Aiden tried to pull her into his arms, but she shrugged him off.

"He knows he has to get his son under control, or he'll lose the election."

She gritted her teeth and suppressed a scream. "God, for a smart man, you're not thinking. You don't get to make choices that can have me and Kellyn silenced forever."

The valet pulled the car around. Aiden opened

the door, and Marina climbed inside. She was so angry. Once again, the Caswells had ruined everything. Only this time, they'd made Aiden their method of delivery.

He pulled out of the parking lot and onto the highway. "I *was* thinking, and that's why I paid him a visit. If one person knows—a person like me—then you'll never be silenced because I'm your echo. I'll always be able to tell your story. Isn't it bad enough that Craig silenced his daughter through terror? The family silenced you. I won't allow them to rule my life, and right now, Marina, you're part of my life. I won't stand by quietly and let them ruin it."

She stared out the window as quiet as her daughter the rest of the way home. When he pulled into his driveway, she hopped out of the car before it stopped and ran to her house. This wasn't how she'd imagined her night would end.

Angry.

Alone.

Afraid.

CHAPTER TWENTY

He was on his third beer when he saw the lights in her house go dark. Had he screwed up everything by stepping in to make sure someone did something?

He'd made the appointment with the mayor as a courtesy, one that told him Aiden wouldn't blink an eye to arrest his son if he showed up anywhere in Aspen Cove. Marina's and Kellyn's safety and security were his number one priority. That was his only objective.

They weren't even a thought in Mayor Caswell's mind. Aiden had spent thirty minutes with the man, and not once did he ask about his granddaughter. He could understand his disregard for Marina, but his own flesh and blood? All the man cared about was his position in the community.

He replayed the whole night over and over in his mind. It had been perfect until the mayor and his wife showed up. Was it a coincidence that they'd picked the same restaurant? He couldn't say. McKinnon's Steakhouse was the best place to eat in Copper Creek, but it wasn't the only place.

He finished his beer and went into the house to climb into his empty, cold bed. The same bed he should have been making love to Marina in. He'd had plans for her. Plans that included lots of pulse-pounding pleasure, slow kisses, and words of love.

As his lids grew heavy, he made a final promise to himself and to Marina. He'd fight to get her back.

"WHO PISSED IN YOUR WHEATIES?" Mark asked. "I thought it would be a great day after your date last night."

Aiden kicked against his desk, forcing his chair to roll back against the wall. "The date was great. The rest...not so much."

Mark widened his eyes. "Hey, man, we all have poor performance days." He chuckled and shuffled the papers on his desk.

"Screw you. I'm not talking about my sex life with you."

"You mean your lack of a sex life." Mark went to the mini-fridge in the corner to get a bottle of water. It had been a hot day with more record heat expected in the weeks to come.

"You remember the restraining order you found while you were snooping?"

Mark twisted the cap from his bottle and took a long drink. "You mean the records I found that you said you wouldn't look at but somehow got filed in your drawer? Yes, I remember that."

"He's not abiding by the order."

Mark plopped back into his chair and wiped his mouth with the back of his hand. "So, let's arrest him."

"Can't. He's out of our jurisdiction, and there's no way his brother will put him in jail."

"Never thought about that. So basically, the restraining order is useless. Just a meaningless piece of paper."

"Exactly. Marina knows too much about that family." Aiden wouldn't give the details to Mark because that would be a breach of trust. "I think they have a be-on-the-lookout for her."

Mark leaned forward. "No way, the town has a BOLO on Marina? For what purpose?"

Aiden shrugged. "Can't say."

His deputy gave him a suspicious look. "You mean you won't say."

"Kind of the same thing in this case." He told Mark about how he'd paid the mayor a visit and how the mayor and his wife showed up for dinner at the same place. He also talked about Craig showing up at the place where Marina was with Kellyn and everything else he could share without breaking his trust with Marina.

"You have so much sucking up to do."

"Says the man who doesn't date."

"I date." He looked around the room like he wanted to escape. "It's just I've got my sights set on someone."

Aiden chuckled. "Better not be Poppy Dawson. Her dad came in and said he didn't want you near his daughter. What's the problem there?"

"The guy is crazy. He holds a grudge against my family." Mark looked at the empty desk in the corner—the one Poppy sat at when she was here. "Hard to avoid someone you work with."

"That's pretty much what I told him."

As if their conversation had conjured her presence, Poppy walked in. She stared at Mark for a moment before her attention returned to Aiden. "Is there anything special you need done?"

Aiden slid a pile of paperwork her way. "These need to be filed, and can you organize things around here?" He looked at Mark. "His system of filing isn't all that effective."

She faced Mark. "What's your system?"

Poppy had dressed extra nice today. Normally she wore slacks and a shirt, but today she was in a pretty sundress. Could be the heat, but that didn't explain the rest. While Poppy wore little makeup, today her cheeks were rosy, and her lips shined.

"Yeah, Mark. Why don't you tell her what your system is?"

Mark let out a disgruntled huff. He pointed to the first pile on his desk. "I've got a now pile." He set his hand on the second pile. "This is a later pile." He straightened the third and largest pile. "This is the if-I-ever-get-time pile."

She breezed over to his desk and swept off the stacks into her hands. "I'll sort them out, then prioritize and alphabetize."

Aiden rose and picked up his hat. "Now that sounds reasonable." He strode to the doorway. "See you kids later. Call me if you need anything."

"Happy sucking up," Mark teased.

Aiden heard Poppy ask what that meant before he walked out. Mark would never tell. He was a good man and could be trusted.

Out of the corner of his eye, he caught the flash of Marina's white SUV down by the park. He wasn't sure if she'd had enough time to get over her anger, but he needed to see her.

He sat in his cruiser for several minutes, watching them play on the swings. When Kellyn jumped off to join the Williams kids in the sandbox, he approached Marina under the big oak tree.

She shaded her eyes with one hand and looked up. "I was wondering if you would sit there all day." She pulled her damp T-shirt away from her skin. "It's a hot one out here."

"We barely have a breeze." He pointed to the space beside her. "Can I sit down?"

"You're asking? I thought maybe you'd just do what you wanted."

By her response, she wasn't over being angry with him. He took a seat and leaned against the trunk of the tree. "I deserve that. I'm sorry." He pulled a wildflower from the ground and plucked the petals off.

"You don't have to get to the end to know she still loves you."

He tossed the half-spent flower aside and threaded his fingers with hers. "By *her*, I'm hoping you mean you."

"You got another *her* that might love you hanging around in the background?"

He looked at Kellyn playing in the sand. "Maybe, but she's never told me."

Marina leaned her head on Aiden's shoulder. "Yet, but she'll get there."

He pulled her hand to his lips and kissed it. "I really am sorry. I was trying to help. I realize that I should have asked you if you wanted help. I assumed it was my job to protect you."

"Aiden, it's not that I didn't want your help, but I know these people. Don't think for a second that the mayor didn't know Craig was harassing me. Hell, Craig used his father's phone to call me."

Aiden had forgotten about that. "I messed up, but I promise I won't step into your business again. It's hard for me to stand back and watch them intimidate you. I see the fear in your eyes when their names come up."

She gripped his biceps and hugged him tightly. "I have to save myself. If I don't, then I'll never find my power. At the ball pit, I did it. I stood up for myself. That was a first for me. It was an empowering feeling. I didn't make a scene because I didn't want Kellyn to see him."

"How did she not see him?"

"She buries herself under the balls for minutes." She shook her head. "I can't imagine what's under those things—how many petrified burgers and fries are on the floor, but she likes it. There are so few glorious moments in her life that I embrace it."

"She's lucky to have a mom like you."

"I'm the lucky one."

"No." He lifted her chin and looked into her eyes. "I'm the lucky one. I'm so sorry I was short-sighted. I don't want this to come between us. Can you forgive me?"

"Already done. I think maybe we were just moving too fast."

His heart stopped and then thudded back to life. "You want to take a step back?" He didn't. He wanted to go full steam ahead. He held his breath, waiting for an answer.

When she frowned, he knew it was coming. "I'm a mess, Aiden. I've been telling you that since the day we met."

He cupped her cheek. "And I've been telling you you're a beautiful mess. You're my mess, Marina. Please don't push me away. I need you as much as I hope you need me." He turned toward Kellyn. "I need her too."

"I don't want to step back, but I think we should slow it down."

It was a compromise, but hell, weren't most things in life? "What does that mean?"

She smiled. "It probably means that we shouldn't be picking out our china patterns this week."

He wrapped his arms around her and tugged her into his lap. "I can wait another week for that."

She gave him a playful punch. "You're impossible."

"Yes, I've heard that, but I'm your impossible, and that makes everything possible."

They sat in companionable silence until Kellyn looked up and saw him there.

She wasted no time in running straight into his arms.

"Hey, Sprout, are you having fun?"

Kellyn buried her head in his neck and held on to him like he might disappear. When she pulled back, she nodded. Her hand came to her lips in her sign language equivalent to *I'm hungry*.

"I should feed her." Marina looked at her phone. "It's way past our normal lunchtime."

Aiden stood with Kellyn in his arms. "I'd like to take you to the diner. If we hurry, we can catch them before they close."

"You're always buying us food."

"I like taking care of you. It gives me purpose. What do you say?" He said a silent prayer that the answer would be yes. He knew the minute Kellyn nodded, he'd won because if Kellyn was communicating, she'd get what she wanted. Then again, she didn't ask for much.

"It's a date," Marina said. She lifted on her tiptoes and pressed a kiss to his lips. Kellyn pressed one to his cheek.

Aiden was overwhelmed with happiness. "Let's take the cruiser and turn on the lights and siren."

Marina widened her eyes. "Are you sure that's wise? What if she always wants to ride with the lights and siren? Besides, it's so close we could walk."

"It's so little to ask."

Marina sidled up to him. "What do I get?"

He didn't miss a beat. He shifted Kellyn to his hip and leaned down to whisper in Marina's ear. "A do-over for last night. I had so many plans."

They got Kellyn's booster seat from the SUV.

"I'm sorry, Aiden. I really screwed it all up."

He opened the door for Marina. "No, you taught me a valuable lesson."

She pulled on her seat belt while Aiden buckled Kellyn in. "What was the lesson?"

"That I don't always know what's right. I should ask before I assume."

"You should also know that I don't want you to stop caring."

"Never, sweetheart." He climbed inside and started the engine. "Are you ready?" He flipped the switch, and the sirens and flashing lights turned on.

Kellyn smiled and clapped her hands. It took so little to make her happy. By the look on Marina's face, she was happy too.

CHAPTER TWENTY-ONE

Had it really been ten days since their failed date?

Marina packed a few more items into the picnic basket. Today was the grand opening of the new fire station, and she had promised Kellyn they could visit and then go to the movie in the park.

She shoved in as many drinks as the container would hold. They'd been in a heat wave for almost two weeks, and she didn't want to risk dehydration.

Without air-conditioning, the only relief they got was the gentle evening breeze that moved through the open windows to cool off the house. She hated to leave them open, but there wasn't much to steal. Aiden reminded her that criminals weren't picky, but it was a choice between letting someone steal what little they had and dying from heatstroke. The options weren't great.

He'd invited them to stay in his home, but she didn't feel right sleeping with Aiden in front of her daughter. Kellyn still didn't speak, so she couldn't be certain she'd understand that dynamic of their relationship. Hell, she didn't understand it. All she knew was her life was better because Aiden was in it. As silly as it seemed, she was in love with him. He was the one for her, and she knew it deep in her bone-marrow.

"Hey, Ladybug, are you ready?" she called from the kitchen. "Aiden said he'd see us at the fire station."

Kellyn came out wearing khaki shorts and a brown T-shirt. On her head was one of Aiden's old sheriff hats. She'd become his mini-me. If he was gardening, so was she. If he was swinging, so was she. If he was trying to kiss Marina, so was she.

"You look very professional, Sheriff."

Kellyn adjusted her cap and smiled.

"Is Mrs. Beasley coming?"

She shook her head. She'd been leaving her emotional crutches behind one by one. It was such a beautiful sight to see her grow and become confident in her new world.

"Let's hit it." They climbed into the SUV and

drove to the fire station, which wasn't far from the park.

It looked like all the kids from Aspen Cove were there climbing on the new fire truck. Chief Mosier supervised while his crew gave fire safety demonstrations and handed out plastic firemen hats.

Aiden and Mark had the cruisers open so people could see inside. The kids had a blast turning on the sirens and lights. Just before they closed the doors, they invited everyone in to slide down the pole. There weren't many adult takers, but the kids had fun.

Marina, Aiden, and Kellyn walked to the park, where they found a perfect spot in front of the in-flatable screen that Samantha and Katie had rented. It was a double feature with two kids' movies playing back-to-back.

Kellyn made it through the first movie and half of the second before she fell asleep.

Aiden carried her to the SUV while Marina was in charge of the empty picnic basket. At home, Marina left Kellyn in the car while she said goodbye to Aiden. They had plans to go to Copper Creek together tomorrow.

Craig hadn't been seen or heard from since the day she'd stood up for herself. Maybe Aiden's influence with the mayor had helped.

She understood his desire to go with them to Kellyn's dentist appointment. Craig was unpredictable and unpredictable was dangerous.

"I'll see you in the morning." Aiden tugged her tightly to his chest and gave her a kiss that warmed her insides. They hadn't been able to schedule their do-over, so it was stolen moments like this that whet their appetites but in no way sated their needs.

"I'll be out front waiting." She leaned forward and breathed him in. She loved the smell of him, and his citrus scent gave her strength. She made sure to rub against him every night so his cologne was fresh on her skin and locked into her senses when she went to bed. She'd almost asked him to spritz her pillow, but didn't because it felt silly when he was only next door.

"I love you," he told her. She loved the way he said it several times a day, so she could never forget how much he truly meant those words. He'd told Kellyn too. Each time he said the words, she pressed her hand to her chest and then to his. There was no doubt she reciprocated the feelings.

"I should get her into bed. She's wiped out." How could she not be after playing for hours?

"You want me to carry her inside?"

Marina shook her head. If he came inside, she knew she'd invite him to stay. Each time they said goodnight, it was harder to walk away and close the door.

"No, I can get her." She gave him another kiss before she got Kellyn and made her way into the house.

Thankfully it was cool. A soft breeze blew the curtains. She breathed in and stopped cold. There was a smell in the air that was frighteningly familiar, but when she looked around the living room, everything was normal.

She shook off the feeling and pressed her nose into Kellyn's hair, who also smelled like Aiden. "Let's go, sweetheart. It's time for bed."

She walked into her room to find Mrs. Beasley sitting in the center of the bed. It was an odd placement since Kellyn was usually so adamant she sit in the rocker, but she'd been excited to leave the house today, so maybe Kellyn hadn't taken the time to put her away.

Marina laid her down and moved Mrs. Beasley to the rocker. She returned to her daughter with pajamas in her hand. It didn't take long to get her changed and tucked into bed. Her tired little eyes opened long enough to convey her happiness.

"You're right. It was a great day." Marina tucked the sheet under her chin and gave her one last kiss. "See you in the morning." She left the room, closing the door halfway behind her.

Marina made her way to the kitchen to clean up from the lunches she'd made. She took a beer from the refrigerator and walked into the living room. Once again, the smell of Craig's cologne washed over her. She knew it was ridiculous, and she hated that she gave his memory life in her mind. He didn't deserve even the tiniest bit of thought.

She'd just flopped onto the couch when the hair stood up on the back of her neck, and she knew it wasn't her imagination.

"Did you really tell him you love him?" His voice echoed from the dark corner of the living room. Vicious intent dripped from each word. The curtains billowed, and he stepped from behind them. "You can't love him if you love me."

Her fear turned into rage. She swallowed a lump of hysteria big enough to choke her. *Victor, not a victim. Victor, not a victim,* she chanted to herself. She tucked her nose into her shoulder to breathe in Aiden.

"Yes," she said with conviction. "I love him." She jumped from the couch, knocking her beer bottle to the ground, and sprinted to the door. The sound of broken glass moved through the silent house. She prayed that Kellyn was so tired she wouldn't hear it.

Her fingers reached for the doorknob but slid

away when he grabbed her hair and yanked her back.

This was it. She had to fight or die, and she had way too much to live for.

He turned her around and pinned her to the wall with one hand at her shoulder and another at her neck.

Movement from the side caught their attention.

"Kellyn, honey. Go back to bed. Mommy will take care of this."

Her little mouth hung open like she was in the middle of a silent scream.

Fury filled Marina.

"Dammit, get your ass to bed!" Craig yelled. "Don't forget, you're not allowed to say a single word."

Kellyn turned around and ran.

All Marina cared about was getting her out of the room, so she saw nothing.

"She doesn't speak because of you." Marina had had enough. She was a mama bear, and she'd do anything to protect her cub. There was no doubt that once Craig was finished with her, he intended to move to her baby. That wasn't happening tonight.

"Unlike you, she's smart and listens." He tightened his hand on her neck, and spots danced in front of her eyes. It was do or die.

She'd learned in self-defense that if she let her body go to goo and fall to the floor, she'd have a chance to get away. She needed those few seconds to prepare.

She collapsed to the floor and rolled away. Craig stood stunned.

Marina popped to her feet. "Are you ready?" She fisted up.

"Ready for what?"

"To have the shit beat out of you." She nailed him in the nose on the last word and didn't let up until he was on his knees, begging for her to stop.

"I begged you, and you never stopped." She delivered a kick she hoped he'd feel for days.

"Mar Mar, stop. You're going to kill me."

She pulled back her foot and nailed him in the hip. It was his favorite place to kick her. Hurt like a bitch for a long time, and it bruised where no one was likely to see it.

"Then so be it. It's a make-my-day state, and you're breaking the restraining order." She delivered a few more blows before she stepped back. "You're a coward. Get up and fight me. You're being bested by a woman."

Craig lay curled in a ball at her feet. The man cried and begged for mercy, but Marina wasn't feeling sympathetic.

CHAPTER TWENTY-TWO

Aiden had traded his uniform for a pair of sweats and a T-shirt. He'd settled into the sofa to watch a movie when someone pounded on his door. He heard a wail that sounded more like a wounded animal than a person.

He flung the door open to find Kellyn dressed in her pajamas, her red block in her hand. This time she wasn't silent. Her tears came with sounds and words.

"He...he kill Mommy again."

Aiden's heart fell to the hardwood floors. "I've got you." He picked Kellyn up and put her on the couch. "I don't want to leave you here, but I have to so I can save your mom. You stay here, okay? I love you. I will take care of you and your mom. I promise."

She took in a jagged breath and curled into the corner of the couch, pulling the throw over her head. "Peas help Mommy."

"I will, baby, I will." Aiden slipped on his shoes and grabbed his service weapon before he shot out of the house like a bullet. He didn't even take the time to call for backup, which was stupid, but Marina didn't have time if she was fighting off Craig.

When he got to the door, her yell wasn't filled with fear but pure anger. Aiden found the door locked and kicked it open. He stopped to take in the scene in front of him. Marina stood with her foot on Craig's neck, and she was choking the life out of him.

He had two choices. He could turn around and let her kill him, or he could tell her to stand aside. He'd made the blunder of choosing for her once before. He wouldn't make that mistake again.

When Marina saw him, she eased the pressure on her foot.

"Thank God," Craig wheezed. "She's trying to kill me."

Aiden appraised the situation. Nothing but a beer bottle was broken. He gave Marina a visual once-over. She was solid and unharmed except for the bruise blooming on her neck. Aiden pointed his weapon at Craig. "Don't move even a fraction of an inch, or I'll shoot you."

"I'm unarmed. You can't shoot me."

Aiden ignored him and walked to Marina. "Hey, sweetheart. You okay?" He glanced down at Craig. "Tough night?"

She laughed. It wasn't a fun laugh, but a laugh of disbelief. "Oh, you know, same old, same old."

Craig lay there bleeding on her floor. No doubt he had a broken nose. By the wheezing in his lungs, probably a few broken ribs. Maybe a punctured lung and one of his fingers wasn't right; it was bent at an odd angle, and he'd never been so proud of Marina.

"You know I love you, and I respect your right to choose for yourself." He leaned in and kissed her cheek without taking his weapon off the asshole. "Should I stay and call for backup, or do you want to finish what you started?" Anger bubbled under Aiden's skin. "Maybe I should kill him for you." He made a show out of checking his weapon, even though he'd chambered the bullet before he entered the house. "Yep, loaded and ready."

Craig scurried back.

Marina shook her head as if she was clearing her thoughts. "You'd kill him for me?"

"Honey, I'd do anything for you. You want him dead?" Aiden hadn't ever stepped outside the law, but he'd do it for Marina and Kellyn. It wouldn't be too hard to prove that Craig came after him. Colorado was a make-my-day state, which meant it was legal to kill an intruder.

She lifted her foot like she might crush his skull. "You do love me, don't you?"

"I do." He looked toward the busted door. "I hate to hurry you up, but our girl is in my house. She's crying, and she asked me to save you."

"She is our girl, Aiden." Marina set her foot down. "How'd she get to your house? Is she okay?"

He shrugged. "I think she climbed out of the window. She'd be better if you were there with her."

"She's not your girl," Craig cried.

Marina kicked him again. "Shut up, or I'll kill you." She pressed a kiss to Aiden's lips. She looked at Craig and growled. "I've got to go. I'll call for backup. Don't kill him. He doesn't deserve an easy death."

"You got it, babe."

She ran out of the house.

"Would you have killed me?" Craig asked from his place on the floor.

Aiden said, "Yes, without a second thought because a man should protect his family. A real man would do anything for his woman, including killing a worthless, spineless piece of shit. She spared you for now."

Craig tried to smile, but his lips were swelling, which made his grin grotesque. "I won't do time. My father would never allow it."

Aiden pressed his weapon to Craig's temple. It would be so easy to pull the trigger, but that wasn't what Marina wanted. It wasn't what he wanted either. His father had raised him to be a better man, but he also had raised him to protect what was his and what was important. In this situation, the two conditions warred with each other.

Seconds later, the sirens of Mark's cruiser filled the air.

He crept to the door with his weapon drawn. "You okay, boss?"

"Never been better."

"I need an ambulance. I'm injured," Craig whined.

Aiden palmed his own chin, his shadow of whiskers scratching against his skin. "Did you ever call an ambulance for Marina?" He turned to Mark. "Call him an ambulance and tell them to pick him up in about an hour at the station. We'll need a bus from Silver Springs."

"No!" Craig yelled. "I want to go to Copper Creek."

Mark handed Aiden his cuffs. Once Craig was

secure, he lifted him to his feet. "You lost your right to choose."

Aiden had Craig secured in a cold, lonely cell and made some calls to ensure he didn't slip through the cracks.

He arrived back home two hours later to find the most beautiful sight he'd ever seen. Marina and Kellyn were tucked in his bed, sound asleep. His keys jingled when he set them on the nightstand.

Marina opened her eyes. "I'm sorry. I couldn't bring her back there. Not until the door is fixed, and it's cleaned up."

He didn't want them to go back there. "Marina, this is where you belong."

She patted the mattress beside her, and he climbed in next to them. His arms circled them both, and he breathed her in. She was coconuts and honey. And she was fierce; he'd never felt so proud in his life. He fell asleep knowing that this was it for him. He would give up everything for them.

AIDEN WOKE to a giggle and the weight of a four-year-old on his stomach. He opened his eyes. "Good morning, little monkey. I'm so proud of you."

He ruffled her hair and waited. God, he hoped she'd found her voice for good.

She poked him in the chest. "I'm poud of you. I wuv you."

Aiden hadn't cried in years, but those seven words meant more to him than anything. He pulled her to his chest and cried into her hair.

Marina rolled over and wrapped her arms around them both. "She's remarkably okay. I'm okay. You're okay. We're going to be okay."

He squeezed them back. "Yes, we are." There was no doubt of the truth of that statement.

HE WOULD HAVE LOVED to take the day off, but there were too many things to do. A door to repair. A living room to clean. Most importantly, he had to make sure that the long arms of Mayor Caswell couldn't reach his son. One of the late-night calls Aiden had made was to a friend who was also a judge. He'd explained the situation and asked if all proceedings could be moved to Silver Springs. Turned out the saying "it's not what you know but who you know" was true. Also true was how karma came around to bless a person or curse them. In Aiden's case, he'd done a favor for Judge Trumble a few years ago, and the man was happy to repay him.

"I've got to go to work for a little while, but why don't we meet back here for lunch?"

Kellyn let out a litany of yeses before she asked for hotdobs and kips. Having been silent for so long, her words weren't clear, but Marina and he understood her completely.

He left the girls at home and went to the office. According to Mark, Craig was handcuffed to his hospital bed. That was a relief, but something about Kellyn's first real words rattled him. "He kill my mommy again." It was the word *again* that shook him to his core.

He spent the morning looking into the disappearance of the first Mrs. Caswell. Kari hadn't been seen in over two years. There wasn't any record of employment, car registration, or credit cards. No paper trail of any kind existed.

The one thing about kids was they didn't play with words. They were literal.

While Marina made him coffee this morning, she'd told him that Craig had told Kellyn she wasn't allowed to say one word, and that was why she didn't.

What was he trying to silence? The only thing that made sense was she saw him kill her mother. He wasn't ready to tell Marina what he knew in his heart. He needed to mull it over—to make sure. Besides, it would take time to get a search warrant for the Caswell house, but he wouldn't stop until he got one and put Craig away for life.

WHEN HE GOT HOME, Marina was there, but Kellyn was gone.

"Where's the little monkey?"

Her smile captivated him. "You know how small towns are. Word gets out, and everyone wants to help. Katie invited the little chatterer over to make cookies."

"Is she okay? I thought she'd be more traumatized. Maybe we should take her to see her therapist."

"I already made the appointment and canceled the dentist for today. We're in Copper Creek all day next Wednesday." She tilted her head back and looked into his eyes. "Dr. Thayer said to let her play this out. She saw Craig in handcuffs being put into the police car. I told her you saved us both, and Craig can never hurt us again. She trusts me. She trusts you. Besides, she loves baby Sahara, so it looks like you're stuck with me."

"I can think of worse scenarios." He ran the pads of his fingers over the bruises on her neck. "Does it hurt?" Seeing the marks made him wish he'd killed the bastard.

She nodded. "But I know how you can make it feel better."

"Is that right?" He hardly recognized the low,

throaty growl that came from his mouth. It was love mixed with relief and need.

"Yes," she said in a breathy whisper.

"I promised you a do-over."

She held his hand and led him toward the bedroom.

"And you're a man of your word."

CHAPTER TWENTY-THREE

"Oh my God," she moaned.

Aiden paused mid-thrust. "Sweetheart. I aim to please." He rolled his hips and pressed forward. When he used the word *aim*, it wasn't wordplay. He knew the exact place to put pressure to send her over the edge for the third time that afternoon.

Her body was boneless as the climax rolled through her. "Aiden...good God."

He collapsed to his elbows, cupping her head between his forearms. The pace of his lovemaking didn't slow or stop, and his hips moved with precision to build her up again.

"I love you, Marina. I could have lost you last night before I made things right. Had the opportunity to show you how much I care about you."

She gripped his hips and pulled him deep inside her. "I know you love me. You don't have to show me how much in one day." She wiped the sweat from his brow. "It's your turn."

"I never thought I'd see the day when a woman said she'd had enough orgasms."

"Is that what you heard?" She pushed his chest, rolling him off her and taking his position on top. "I'll never have enough of you. I'll never reach my limit of pulse-pounding, heart-stopping climaxes, but you've given enough for today."

She lined herself above him and slid slowly onto his hardness. Watching his eyes nearly roll back into his head and hearing him groan was the greatest reward.

He set his hands on her hips. "I promise to always give more than I take."

She raised and lowered again and again.

"Oh holy hell." His hips moved under hers. She picked up the pace until he couldn't take it anymore. "Marina, I'm...I'm—"

"I know, let it go." She pressed into him and stilled. His head moved from side to side as he peaked and fell over the edge with words of love on his lips.

They lay sated in each other's arms, facing one another. She knew from the look on his face that he had questions. Questions that didn't belong in their bed.

"Let's get up. I can see an interrogation coming."

He pulled her close and kissed her. "Not really. I was admiring your strength. Who knew my woman was such a badass?"

She rolled out of bed and put on his shirt. It hung nearly to her knees. "Out of bed, buster. There isn't room for anything between those sheets but love, great sex, and sleep."

When he stood, her eyes went from his shoulders to the heavy length between his legs. He was a beautiful man—tall and proud and hung. He was everything she'd dreamed a man should be—kind, gentle, loving.

He looked at the mussed-up bed. "It was great, wasn't it?"

She brushed her fingers across his chest as she passed him on her way to the kitchen. "Best I've ever had."

He stepped into his jeans and pulled them up. "Best you'll ever have, you mean."

He followed her while he put her favorite blue shirt on. "You're sounding confident."

He came up behind her, wrapping his arms around her waist. "Okay, the last I hope you'll ever have, so I'm not so much confident as I am hopeful."

She took a glass from the cabinet and set it on the counter. "My last?" She liked the sound of that. She wanted no one else but him.

"You know where this is going." He turned her around and lifted her to the granite counter. "I won't ask today because it's just too much too soon, but I will ask."

"What do you want to ask me, Aiden?"

He smiled. "You know how I like things to be just right."

She giggled. "I'm nearly naked in your kitchen. What could be more perfect?" She had a feeling about what he wanted to ask, but she wanted to hear the words and know that the man saying them was serious about his intentions.

"Sandwiches sound perfect." He reached above her head and took out a jar of peanut butter. "Damn, woman, you made me hungry."

He moved away from her to get the bread and jelly. While he made sandwiches, she thought about her past.

"You know, he never really asked, and I never loved him."

Aiden's knife stopped halfway through spreading the peanut butter over the bread. "I know. You stayed because of Kellyn."

She nodded. "Yes, but I want you to know that I've never loved anyone like I love you."

237

He dropped the knife and went to her, putting his hands on her thighs. "I'm so happy to hear that, baby. I've loved no one like I love you." He ran his hands up her bare thighs until he reached under the shirt. "Round three or food?"

She gave him a quick kiss and slid off the counter in front of him. "Food, then round three." She looked at the clock. Katie had said she'd bring Kellyn home by five. They had less than an hour left. "Eat up. We don't have much time."

She'd never seen a man wolf down a sandwich so quickly. They didn't make it back to bed. Instead, they took it to his shower where he lathered her body and made her feel clean and dirty at the same time.

Dressed and sitting on the leather sofa like they hadn't made love all afternoon, they waited. Aiden opened his mouth to talk but closed it quickly. He did that several times before Marina reached out and touched his arm.

"You want to ask something?"

He looked at her thoughtfully. "I don't want to ruin the day, but this is important."

She scooted closer to him. "You can ask me anything."

"When you moved into that asshole's house, was there any new construction? Anything that was recently finished?"

While she loved that he called Craig asshole, she didn't understand what he was getting at. "Umm, I'm not sure." She pressed her memory to the first days after she'd moved in to the big house on Pinecone Road. "A neighbor asked me if I was enjoying the new hot tub, but I'm not sure when it went in. It could have been months or years. Why?"

The creases in Aiden's brow deepened. "Kellyn's statement, 'He kill my mommy again' has been bothering me. Her words imply he did it before."

Marina's hand covered her mouth. "Oh God, she's buried in the backyard, and Kellyn knew it. That poor little thing."

Before they could discuss it further, the doorbell rang, and Kellyn was home.

Katie stood beside her with a plate of cookies in her hand. "We brought treats."

"Yep, teats," Kellyn mimicked.

Aiden picked Kellyn up and swung her in a circle. "You brought me treats?"

She nodded. "Do we have to share them with Mommy?" Kellyn nodded again.

Aiden looked at Katie. "Thanks for taking her and giving Marina and me some time."

"You bet," Katie said. "Looks like she found her voice and is making up for lost time."

Marina laughed. "Talked your ear off?"

"Not really, but I think she likes hearing her

voice. I know I do." She waved to where Aiden and Kellyn sat eating cookies. "See you later, Coop," Katie said before she left.

Marina approached her two favorite people in the world.

"Coop?" Kellyn tilted her head in confusion.

Aiden pointed to himself. "Aiden Cooper."

Kellyn pointed to herself. "Kellyn Cooper."

Aiden looked at Marina, then back at Kellyn. "Yes, sweetie. That's the plan."

She wasn't sure she could fall more in love with the man, but right then, when he gave her daughter his promise, she knew he was right: he'd be her last. And as odd as it sounded, he was her first. The first man she'd truly loved.

CHAPTER TWENTY-FOUR

It didn't take much to get the search warrant. A few calls and probable cause had a forensic crew at the Caswell house within days. They took three more days to find Kari Caswell's remains buried under the hot tub. Craig Caswell wouldn't bother anyone else for the rest of his life.

Each day a new news crew showed up until the street was full of reporters. It was a media circus not even the Copper Creek police chief could contain. Mayor Caswell was suspiciously absent, but then again, it was only weeks before the election, and he couldn't be involved in a scandal.

Aiden leaned back in his chair and waited for his new deputy to arrive. When Kellyn came running inside, he pulled over the chair he'd bought for her and sat her down next to him. On her chest, she had a name tag that read *Kellyn Cooper*. On the second line, in smaller letters, it read *deputy sheriff in training*. He was determined to erase anything Caswell from her life. As soon as he could change her name, he would.

"You ready to work?"

"Yep." She opened the drawer he'd given her and took out her crayons and paper.

Mark walked inside. "Hey, Kellyn, are you sketching a suspect?"

She focused on the paper as she drew. "Yep."

He took his seat and smiled. "Aiden, are you ever going to—"

"Yep. When the timing is perfect."

Kellyn hopped off her chair and brought her sketch to Mark. He laughed. "That's awesome." He brought his hand to his mouth and made a crackling sound like he was talking into a radio. "Attention all officers, be on the lookout for a daisy with a rogue ladybug driving it." He held up the picture Kellyn had drawn. It was a big yellow daisy with a ladybug in the center.

"You're silly," she said. She opened his drawer and got the tape. Behind him, she found an empty spot on the wall next to her pictures of swing sets and stick families that had a mom, a dad, and a little brown-haired girl.

Aiden rose from his chair. "Hold down the fort. Kellyn and I have plans."

Marina had a busy day at the shop. She was doing two perms and a color, which meant she couldn't keep as close an eye on Kellyn as she'd like, but Aiden didn't mind. He loved spending time with his little deputy.

"Where are you two off to?"

Aiden smiled. "We're off to create perfection."

Mark's mouth hung open.

"Close your mouth before you catch flies."

"Good luck, man."

He had everything planned. There would be no rose petals leading to the bedroom. No bubble bath and champagne with a ring at the bottom of the flute. Kellyn had chosen the menu for the night, and no surprise: it was hotdobs and kips.

"Hey, Monkey, let's get ice cream for tonight."

Nothing excited her more than a trip to Sam's Scoops. He didn't care what flavor they had. He was renaming them anyway. When they arrived at Sam's, they stood in front of the window, and Sam said, "I've got—"

"Hey, Sam, we'll take one of each, extra ants." Sam didn't blink an eye at the rude interruption. He didn't care as long as he got the sale.

With their three containers of ice cream, they headed back home. Kellyn put on her prettiest dress, and Aiden put on his new jeans and Marina's favorite shirt. It wasn't fancy, but it was them, and it was perfect.

At ten minutes after five, she walked inside the door. She'd been staying mostly at her place because of Kellyn. But they ate at his house every night because he had a better kitchen and air-conditioning. They didn't get many intimate moments, but they snuck them in when they could. He owed Louise, Katie, and Sage a lot for taking Kellyn for long lunches and overnights.

Many would think they were rushing things, but he didn't want to wait another minute to make them a family.

"Hey," she said. "How are my two favorite people?"

She gave her daughter a kiss and then walked to Aiden, who was putting hotdogs on a plate.

"We're grilling hotdogs, Kellyn. That's so exciting."

"We have ice cweam too," she added.

"Ooh, ice cream." She started toward the freezer. "What flavors did he have today?"

Aiden closed the door before she could look inside. "You know the rule, you have to eat dinner before dessert."

He loved the way Marina's lip rolled forward into a pout. "But I love Malted Mazel Tov."

He rubbed his thumb across her lip. "I promise to put a smile on your face later."

"Last minute sleepover?" she asked with excitement in her voice.

"Sorry, we'll have to make tonight perfect with what we've got, which is hotdogs, chips, Sam's Scoops, and us."

"Yay," Kellyn called out as she ran past them into the backyard.

"Help me grill?" Aiden took two beers from the refrigerator, popped the tops, and handed one to Marina.

"Anything for you."

"I'll remember that."

He put the dogs on the preheated grill. It didn't take long for them to cook. He called out to Kellyn that dinner was ready.

"That was quick. Are you sure they're ready?" She turned a few over to see the grill lines.

"They're perfect. Trust me. Everything is perfect." He'd used that word several times since she'd been home, but she was none the wiser.

Dinner was indeed perfect. It was everything he wanted it to be. These were his girls, and this was his family. In a few minutes, he'd make it official.

"Who wants ice cream?"

He laughed as Marina and Kellyn bounced in

their seats. "What flavors did you get?" Marina asked once more.

Aiden went to the freezer and brought out three separate containers. He'd marked them so he could tell them apart. Kellyn's had a daisy. Marina's had a capital P for perfect. If it all went down the way he hoped, his pretty damn good life would get an upgrade.

He sat and shuffled the containers around like he was playing a shell game.

"Who goes first?"

Kellyn shouted, "Me, me, me."

Since she'd found her voice, she never stopped talking, but he never tired of listening to her.

He looked down at the containers and slid hers in front of her. "This one is special. It's called 'Daddy's Little Girl.' It's chocolate ice cream, with marshmallows and chocolate kisses, and this one is extra special because it's only for you, Kellyn." He popped the lid off to show a scoop of ice cream but sitting on top was an inexpensive necklace with a ladybug and a daisy hanging from its silver chain. Once he wiped it off, he kneeled in front of Kellyn and said, "You're as cute as a ladybug and as pretty as a flower. I love you, Kellyn. I'll always love you." He placed it on her neck. Her little fingers touched it like he'd given her life.

He turned to Marina, who was already crying. "Not yet, sweetheart. It's almost your turn."

"Aiden Cooper, if you have a necklace in my ice cream, I will bawl like a baby."

He held her ice cream in his hand. "This one is really special. It's love mixed with a side of happiness and a sprinkle of passion. Not enough passion because we have a four-year-old, but it's got an extra serving of love."

She reached for the covered cup with shaking hands. "All that in one ice cream?"

"And more," he said before he took a knee in front of her. Kellyn hopped down from her chair and stood by her mom. "You gonna help me with this part?"

She nodded.

"What are you doing, Aiden?" Marina's voice shook with each word.

"I told you I had a question to ask when the time was perfect. It's time." He lifted the lid to her ice cream to show her the solitaire sitting on top of the scoop. "Yours is called 'Marry Me Marina.'"

Kellyn looked at the ring. "Pretty."

"Oh my God." She looked at him with love, hope, and tears in her eyes.

He took the ring from the ice cream and cleaned it with his mouth. "Marina, will you marry me? I'm a simple man with a simple job. I'll never be rich in money, but marry me and make me rich in love. The ring isn't as big as you deserve, but my love is huge." He held it at the tip of her ring finger.

"Aiden, it's everything." She pushed her finger forward until the ring was exactly where it should be. "You're everything."

"Yay!" Kellyn said as she threw her hands around their necks and kissed them both.

"Yes," Marina said. "Yes to your question, Aiden, and yes to our perfect family."

Marina picked up her phone and dialed Katie. "Hey, I need a favor."

In minutes, Kellyn was at Katie's watching a movie with Sahara.

Aiden was making love to his fiancée. They only had an hour, but it was perfect.

CHAPTER TWENTY-FIVE

Aiden wanted to go to a justice of the peace the day after he put that ring on her finger, but she wanted more. She wanted to be free of everything so she could give herself to him fully.

Not that she belonged to anyone else, but Craig still owned pieces of her brain, and he would until she knew he'd be locked away forever.

It had been three months since Kellyn spoke more than one word. The Guild Creative Center opened, and Samantha's band came to town. Doc got his straight edge shave and didn't need emergency medical intervention. Summer had turned to fall, and the only heat Marina felt happened between the sheets of Aiden's bed when they managed to get alone time.

A lot had happened in those months. Mayor Caswell lost the election and moved to another state. Police Chief Caswell resigned after it was leaked that he'd ignored a multitude of complaints about his brother. The only Caswell left in a position of power was Conrad, but no one heard a thing from him.

Marina sat in the back of the courthouse in Silver Springs and waited for the verdict. She could have provided the video of him abusing her to add to the case, but she was a woman of her word. She'd traded her story and her right to tell it for a beautiful little girl. She'd make the same decision all over again.

Kellyn would turn five in a week. Weekly speech therapy sessions had proven successful, and she was growing and thriving. The first time she called Aiden Daddy, they smiled and didn't make a big deal of it, but Marina knew how much it meant to him.

The door to the courthouse opened. Aiden walked inside and took the seat beside her. He wore his uniform. She'd never met a man who looked sexier in brown and khaki. Hell, he looked good in anything and better in nothing.

"Any news yet?"

Marina twisted her hands in her lap. "No." She

worried that the time it was taking to come to a verdict wasn't a good sign. "I'm worried that he'll go free." If he did, she'd never be safe.

Aiden turned her to face him. "Sweetheart, they have to decide whether to give him life or death. He'll never get to you or Kellyn again."

She gripped his hands like they were lifelines.

A side door opened, and a guard led Craig into the courtroom. He looked haggard and worn. His eyes lifted to hers, but he immediately looked away. His power was gone. Craig Caswell could no longer hurt her.

Minutes later, the jury arrived.

This was it. She held her breath as they read the verdict. Craig Caswell was guilty of first-degree murder. The jury recommended life.

He deserved the same as what he gave, terror and death, but she had spared him, Aiden had spared him, and the state had spared him. She only hoped the prison system wouldn't be so kind.

She let out a sigh and buried her face in Aiden's chest. It was over. Now her life could begin. When she came to Aspen Cove, she had been certain of three things. Absolute power corrupted absolutely. All the good men were married or dead. And she'd do absolutely anything to protect her daughter.

She was wrong about only one thing. There

were still good men out there, and she'd found the best of the bunch when she moved next door to Aiden.

CHAPTER TWENTY-SIX

TWO WEEKS LATER

Aiden stood under the covered pavilion at Hope Park, waiting for his bride. It was the perfect place to start a new life. It was here where he'd realized she was his everything.

In the distance, he saw Kellyn get out of the car at the curb. She was so pretty in her soft pink dress. She skipped along, tossing daisies at will from the basket she carried. Behind her were his friends. Bowie led Katie. Cannon led Sage. Wes led Lydia.

"You picked yourself a fine one, Sheriff," Doc Parker said. He was the official everything in town and the only one licensed to marry them. He stood in front of Aiden, craning his neck to see who would appear next. When the old man's mustache lifted into a broad smile, Aiden knew Marina was here.

"She's a beauty," Doc remarked.

"She sure as hell is. She's everything."

Kellyn made it to the front and tugged on Aiden's hand. "Do I look pretty, Daddy?"

He leaned down and kissed her cheek. "You are the prettiest five-year-old I know." He turned her around to look toward her mom, who was dressed in a simple white gown. "Here comes Mommy."

Marina didn't want the big wedding and the white dress until he reminded her that she'd never technically been married. Since this was the only time she'd get married, it should be special.

She made her way across the lawn. Her eyes never left his as Mark walked her to Aiden. Tired of waiting, he met her halfway.

"Are you ready?" He covered her hand with his and led her to where Doc waited.

"I'm ready. Today is the first day of the rest of our life together."

Aiden cradled her neck and kissed her.

Doc cleared his throat to get their attention. "I didn't give you permission to kiss her."

They both looked at Doc. "We're long past permission," Aiden added.

Doc leaned in and whispered. "Let me at least

get the words out. You want to hear the words, right?"

They held hands and listened as Doc had them repeat their vows. They were quick. They were simple. They were perfect.

As with any small town, the people provided everything. Under the canopy of the picnic area, dozens of casseroles were uncovered. Samantha's band set up in the corner and provided the music.

Aiden danced with his wife until her feet ached. "Are you ready to go home?"

"I was ready after I said 'I do.'"

Aiden laughed. "What the hell have I been waiting for?"

"I have no idea, Mr. Cooper. Let's say good-night to our daughter and climb into bed."

"Mrs. Cooper, I hope you ate enough because you're going to need energy for the night."

She giggled. "Is that a promise?"

"Nope, it's a guarantee."

Aiden's mom had come up for the wedding, as had Marina's. They were staying at the bed and breakfast and were taking Kellyn for a sleepover. As soon as Aiden and Marina kissed everyone goodbye, he carried his wife to the waiting Mustang.

Lloyd Dawson stopped him before he could drive away.

"Sorry to bother you, Sheriff, but have you seen Poppy?"

"Last time I saw her, she was listening to the band." Aiden pointed to the pergola.

As they drove down Main Street, he noticed the lights in the sheriff's station were on, and a shadow had moved behind the blinds. His deputy was working again. That young man was all work and no play.

Although his bride was in the car, Aiden knew he had to stop and tell Mark to go home or at least go back to the reception.

"Be right back, sweetie."

Marina smiled. "Do your thing. I'm not going anywhere."

Aiden walked through the door expecting to find Mark at his desk, but what greeted him was a surprise. In the corner by the coat rack was Poppy. She had Mark pinned to the wall with a kiss.

Aiden cleared his throat.

The two separated quickly. Red bloomed on Mark's cheeks.

Poppy scrambled back. "Oh, here it is," Poppy said with a shaky voice. She took a sweater from the rack. "Thanks, Mark, for helping me find it."

She lowered her eyes and moved toward the door.

"Your father is looking for you," Aiden said. He

wanted to laugh at the shock on both of their faces, but he shuttered his surprise.

"Shit," Mark blurted. "You should go out the back door."

Poppy looked at Aiden and then back to Mark before she took off at a near run toward the rear exit.

"Hope you know what you're doing," Aiden said to Mark before he turned to leave. As he reached the door, he stopped. "My bride is waiting for me in the car. You better not get shot because I'm not covering for your stupid ass."

Aiden walked out and climbed into the waiting Mustang.

"Everything all right?" Marina asked.

Aiden shook his head, then chuckled. "Everything is perfect."

GET A BONUS SCENE

Do you want to a bonus chapter from One
Hundred Excuses?
Click here to get an extra unpublished scene.

ALSO BY KELLY COLLINS

An Aspen Cove Romance Series

One Hundred Reasons

One Hundred Heartbeats

One Hundred Wishes

One Hundred Promises

One Hundred Excuses

One Hundred Christmas Kisses

One Hundred Lifetimes

One Hundred Ways

One Hundred Goodbyes

One Hundred Secrets

One Hundred Regrets

One Hundred Choices

One Hundred Decisions

One Hundred Glances

One Hundred Lessons

One Hundred Mistakes

One Hundred Nights

One Hundred Whispers
One Hundred Reflections
One Hundred Intentions
One Hundred Chances
One Hundred Dreams

GET A FREE BOOK.

Go to www.authorkellycollins.com

ABOUT THE AUTHOR

International bestselling author of more than thirty novels, Kelly Collins writes with the intention of keeping love alive. Always a romantic, she blends real-life events with her vivid imagination to create characters and stories that lovers of contemporary romance, new adult, and romantic suspense will return to again and again.

For More Information
www.authorkellycollins.com
kelly@authorkellycollins.com

A NOTE FROM THE AUTHOR

Many may ask why this story? When I planted Marina in *One Hundred Reasons*, I had no idea she'd get her own book. My intent was to show Sage's compassion. When I placed her in *One Hundred Wishes*, I knew there was a story to tell when Samantha saw the bruises on Marina's stomach and assumed they were from abuse. Now we know they came from her self-defense classes.

It was then that I knew Marina was not a victim but a victor. She had gone through hell, but she was determined to save her daughter or die trying.

One Hundred Excuses is a book about triumph over tragedy. About how the human spirit can heal, learn to trust, and love again. How the right people can change everything. I hope you loved this book as much as I loved writing it. As with all Aspen Cove books, it was about finding love in the most unlikely places because in Aspen Cove, everything is possible.